The Faery Lifecycle

John Kruse

GREEN MAGIC

The Faery Lifecycle © 2021 by John Kruse. All rights reserved. No part of this book may be used or reproduced in any form without written permission of the author, except in the case of quotations in articles and reviews.

Green Magic
53 Brooks Road
Street
Somerset
BA16 0PP
England

www.greenmagicpublishing.com

Designed and typeset by K.DESIGN
Winscombe, Somerset

ISBN 9781838418526

GREEN MAGIC

Contents

Introduction	5
CHAPTER ONE Fairy Births	7
Mixed Race Children	16
Faery Ointment	25
CHAPTER TWO Faery Childhood and Growth	28
Fairy Children	28
Infant Looks	33
Maturity	34
Older Faeries	36
CHAPTER THREE Faery Physique	37
Corporeal Creatures?	38
Weight	44
Height	45
Strength	52
Motion	55
Hair	55
Skin	59
Eyes	62
Senses	63
Faeries and the Elements	65
Magic	67
Faery Figures	68
Faery Faces	70

Disability and Deformity	76
Sleep	78
Odour	79
Bone Structure	81

CHAPTER FOUR Faery Health — 84
Diet	84
Excretion	90
Intoxication	91
Cleanliness	93
Bathing faes	93
Fairy laundry	95
Maintaining Physical Health	96
Herbs	102
Food	104
Water	105
Rituals and other items	106
Conclusions	107
Mental Health	108

CHAPTER FIVE Faery Mortality — 115
Fairy Immortality	115
Faery Mortality	117
Life Spans	123
Accidental Deaths	124
Faeries Killing Faeries	125
Humans Killing Faeries	126
Suicide	133
Earthly Remains	134

Conclusions — 137

APPENDIX A Note on Faery Herbs — 139

Introduction

In 1959 respected fairy authority Katharine Briggs published a book, *The Anatomy of Puck*. The title suggested a study of the physique of the archetypal English hobgoblin; instead, the book was a study of faery belief in Elizabethan times, as found in the works of Shakespeare, Drayton, Milton and many others.

The Anatomy of Puck is a very important and useful volume, but it made me realise that we lack a text that looks at the actual physicality of fairies – their anatomies, physiologies, even their psychology. This small book hopes to begin to remedy that gap.

As will be obvious, this book is founded squarely upon an acceptance that faeries have a tangible physical reality and that we can describe them medically and biologically, in just the same manner as may be done for any other living being. It is, therefore, to some degree a natural history of faery kind, but it is limited to an examination of their bodies. I have dealt in detail with faery habitat, diets and communities in several other books. The aim of this short text is to bring the corporeal information to the fore.

A display of a faery corpse, allegedly found in 1902, can be enjoyed on-line. This is a very impressive fake, but what this book seeks to do is to get as close as possible to the facts through the recorded testimony of centuries of folk experience. The alleged corpse has wings, for example – in compliance with the preconceptions of modern audiences – but the traditional sources make no mention of wings and, as a result, they will not be discussed in this account.[1]

---

1 http://www.danbaines.com/blog/anatomical-study-of-the-common-fairy/19/4/2018

CHAPTER ONE

Fairy Births

Starting at the very beginning, the Scottish faery authority Robert Kirk declared, in response to the question "Do these airie Tribes procreate?" that:

> "Supposing all Spirits to be created at once in the Beginning, Souls to pre-exist and to circle about into several States of Probationship; to make them either totally unexcusable, or perfectly happie against the last Day, solves all the Difficulties. But in very Deed, and speaking suteable to the Nature of Things, there is no more Absurditie for a Spirit to inform ane Infant in Bodie of Airs, than a Bodie composed of dull and drusie Earth; the best of Spirits have always delyghted more to appear into aereal, than into terrestrial Bodyes…
>
> Now the Air being a Body as well as Earth, no Reason can be given why there may not be Particles of more vivific Spirit form'd of it for Procreation, than is possible to be of Earth, which takes more Time and Pains to rarify and ripen it, ere it can come to have a prolific Virtue. And if our Aping Darlings did not thus procreate, there whole Number would be exhausted after a considerable Space of Time [i.e. by natural

THE FAERY LIFECYCLE

wastage of the population, on which see the final chapter of this book]."[2]

This positive testimony notwithstanding, the evidence that we have indicates that fairy births are few and far between and that the whole business of labour and nursing are problematic for our Good Neighbours. Direct testimony is found in the Cornish story of *The Fairy Dwelling on Selena Moor,* in which human abductee Grace Hutchens informs her former lover, when he asks about faery children, that there are:

> "Very few indeed… though they are fond of babies, and make great rejoicing when one happens to be born amongst them; and then every little man, however old, is proud to be thought the father."[3]

The trows of the Shetland Islands seem to have problems with fertility comparable to those suffered by the Cornish piskies. Their regular thefts of human women arise from the fact that the trows are unable to produce female babies, it is said. Others think that the problems are restricted to the Kunal trows, who take human wives but always lose the mothers as soon as a baby has been born.[4]

The impression of infertility given by Grace Hutchens is certainly reinforced by a late nineteenth century account given by Angus McLeod of Harris. He sadly remarked

---

[2] Kirk, *Secret Commonwealth,* Conclusion, Question 3.
[3] Bottrell, *Traditions and Hearthside Stories of West Cornwall,* vol. 2, 1873, 100.
[4] Nicolson, *Shetland Folklore,* 77.

that "There is not a wave of prosperity upon the fairies of the knoll, no, not a wave. There is no growth or increase, no death or withering upon the fairies. Seed unfortunate they!" A far more recent Scottish witness, from Ross, agreed that the fairies were an ancient people, who were immortal and who did not breed. From Scotland to Cornwall, therefore, there is a belief that the faeries as a people have a low fertility.[5]

Indirect evidence of the difficulties faced during childbirth comes from the frequency with which human midwifes are taken to assist faery mothers. Such episodes are a staple of British folklore, but their focus is always upon the midwife and her accidental acquisition of second sight by applying ointment to her eyes (more of which later). What is rarely commented upon is the fact that there seem to be no faery women with the same skills and that the human midwives always seem to be fetched in an emergency. The absence of faeries able to assist during the delivery of children is odd and demands explanation. Perhaps (as Grace Hutchens stated) pregnancies are so rare that it is neither possible nor necessary to acquire the obstetric skills; perhaps, instead, the faeries think it more efficient to hire-in the help when they require it and instead devote their time to pleasure.

An alternative explanation for the need for skilled human intervention is that childbirth, for some reason, proves particularly perilous to faery females. The ballad of *Leesom Brand* offers some substantiation for this

---

5   Wentz, *Fairy Faith in Celtic Countries*, 116; *www. tobarandualchais.co.uk*, July 1960.

theory: the eponymous hero is a human boy who goes to work as a servant in the faery king's court. He falls for the king's daughter; she gets pregnant and they run away together. During their journey, she goes into labour and:

> "He hasted him to yon greenwood tree,
> For to relieve his gay ladye;
> But found his ladye lying dead,
> Likeways her young son at her head."[6]

Leesom Brand is able to magically revive the mother and child, fortunately. Of course, it's fair to say that at the time of writing the ballad (the fifteenth or sixteenth century) labour was a dangerous experience for all women, both mortal and supernatural; additionally, we have to acknowledge that the mother in this case was very young (like her partner) being only eleven or twelve years old. Even so, there is some indication that childbirth might be a dangerous time for faery mothers; the Cornish story of *Cherry of Zennor* and its various related versions reinforce this: Cherry is offered her position caring for the faery gentleman's baby son precisely because he has recently been widowed.

That faery women might not be especially fertile or suited to motherhood is further implied by the fact that human women newly delivered of children are frequently abducted to act as nurse maids for faery infants. In his renowned book, *The Secret Commonwealth of Elves, Fauns and Fairies,* seventeenth century Scottish minister

---

6   See my *Fairy Ballads*.

Robert Kirk described this process, seemingly from first-hand experience:

> "Women are yet alive who tell they were taken away when in Child-bed to nurse Fairie Children, a lingering voracious Image of them being left in their place... The Child, and Fire, with Food and other Necessaries, are set before the Nurse how soon she enters [i.e. into the faery dwelling]; but she nather perceaves any Passage out nor sees what those People doe in other Rooms of the Lodging. When the Child is wained, the Nurse dies, or is conveyed back, or gets it to her choice to stay there."[7]

Later, Kirk made further comments upon the breast-feeding of faery babes by human mothers:

> "The Pith and Spirits only of Women's Milk feed their Children, being artificially conveyed, (as Air and Oyl sink into our Bodies,) to make them vigorous and fresh. And this shorter Way of conveying a pure Aliment, (without the usuall Digestions,) by transfusing it, and transpyring thorow the Pores into the Veins, Arteries, and Vessells that supplie the Bodie, is nothing more absurd, than ane Infant's being fed by the Navel before it is borne, or than a Plant, which groweth by attracting a livelie juice from the Earth thorow many small Roots and Tendons, whose coarser

---

[7] Kirk, *Secret Commonwealth*, c.4.

> Pairts be adapted and made connatural to the Whole, doth quickly coalesce by the ambient Cold; and so are condens'd and bak'd up into a confirm'd Wood in the one, and solid Bodie of the Flesh and Bone in the other."

We shall have more to say later about the actual manner of faery nourishment from human foodstuffs, but the fact of suckling by human women is unquestioned by Kirk.[8]

An example of human wet-nursing is found in the ballad *The Queen of Elfan's Nourice*. The mortal mother laments to the queen that she has been taken from her home and her own newly born child, but she is told:

> 'O nurse my bairn, nourice,' she says,
> 'Till he stan at your knee,
> An' ye's win hame to Christen land,
> Whar fain it's ye wad be.
> O keep my bairn, nourice,
> Till he gang by the hauld,
> An' ye's win hame to your young son
> Ye left in four nights auld...'

The human is, essentially, captive, until the faery child is old enough to toddle whilst holding her hand; only then will she be allowed to return home to her own son.[9] The folklore records report actual instances of such abductions. In 1647 Barbara Parish of Livingstone described how she had been approached by some fairies looking for a nurse for one of their babies and, in

---
8 Kirk, *Secret Commonwealth,* Conclusion, Question 3.
9 See my *Fairy Ballads*.

FAIRY BIRTHS

response, she had suggested her neighbour. The *Carmina Gadelica* collection of Gaelic songs includes the verse *Crodh Chailean* which was sung by a woman abducted to nurse the human babies stolen by the faeries and who was held by them until Halloween, "when all the bowers were open" and she could be rescued by her husband.[10]

Once again, we must speculate about the faeries' motives for their practice of kidnapping wet nurses. They may be poor at producing sufficient breast milk; they may be wanting in maternal feeling; perhaps, even, the faery queen would rather be feasting with her husband and court than being tied to a cradle and a perpetually hungry infant. The idea that the faeries might consider human care better than their own comes from an incident in Nithsdale where a faery woman entered the home of a human mother nursing her newly born child and asked her to "Gie my bonnie thing a suck." The human agreed, but the faery instantly vanished with the words "Nurse kin' an' ne'er want" ('Nurse kindly and you won't go without'). This promise was fulfilled, by daily gifts of clothes and food.[11]

The last indication that the fairies may be not be very fertile is to be found in another class of abductions. Midwives and wet nurses are taken for the duration of the service they provide; for the former, this is a few hours, or days, at the most, after which they are returned home until required again. The wet nurses appear to be taken against their wills and are kept for months but, as *The Queen of Elfan's Nourice* demonstrates, they receive

---

10 Evans-Wentz, *Fairy Faith,* 98, fn.1; Carmichael, *Carmina Gadelica,* vol.1.
11 R. Cromek, *Remains of Nithsdale & Galloway Song,* 302–3.

a fee, food, lodging and other favours in return before being released. There are, however, human women who are taken permanently and for the purposes of breeding. They may be dignified with the label of 'faery wives,' but the truth generally is that they are abducted solely to provide sexual and maternal services. The folklore offers plenty of examples of such cases: Eilian of Garth Dorwen, in Carmarthenshire, is one such. She was hired by an elderly couple to help on their farm and got into the habit of spinning outside in a meadow by moonlight, where the *tylwyth teg* would visit her. Eventually, Eilian disappeared with the fairies. Later, the farmer's wife, who was a midwife, was called to a birth in a fairy hill and discovered that Eilian was the mother in labour.[12]

In February 1931 a Welsh journal reported the relatively recent case of a district nurse who had quit Rhosmynydd Nursing Committee after a faery encounter. Nurse Pritchard was employed in 1910 and, within a few months, received a call at night to attend a birth. The mother's family were "a throng of dwarfish people," the height of children aged eight or ten, but she recognised the woman in labour as matching the description of a girl called Jenny Evans who had left for school one morning in June 1900 and who had never been seen again. Here she now was, the proud mother of a "small, old, withered elf child." The nurse tried to baptise the new-born and was forcibly expelled by the fairies.[13]

Even more intriguing than the foregoing examples is the story of Katherine Fordyce of Unst, Shetland.

---
12 Rhys, *Celtic Folklore*, 211–212.
13 Dorothea Pugh Jones, 'A Case Not Entered,' *Welsh Outlook*, vol.18(2), February 1931, 45.

FAIRY BIRTHS

Katherine died at the birth of her first child – or so it seemed to her family and friends. However, a neighbour's wife dreamed shortly after Katherine's death that she came to her and said "I have taken the milk of your cow that you could not get, but it shall be made up to you; you shall have more than that, if you will give me what you will know about soon." The good wife would not promise, because she had no idea what Katherine meant or what she was asking for, but soon afterwards she discovered that she was pregnant and understood that it was this child of her own to which Katherine referred. The baby in due course was born and the mother named it Katherine Fordyce. After it was christened the 'trow-bound' Katherine re-appeared to the mother and told her all should prosper in her family whilst the child remained with it. Katherine also told the woman that she was herself quite comfortable among the trows, but could not escape unless somebody chanced to see her in the trow's hill and had presence of mind enough to call on God's name. She said her friends had failed to sain her (guard her by spells) at the time of her own child's birth, and that was how she had fallen into the power of the trows.

Later, a man named John Nisbet saw Katherine. He was walking near her old home, when it seemed as if a hole opened in the side of a faery knowe. He looked in and saw Katherine inside, sitting in a "queer-shaped armchair and nursing a baby." There was a bar of iron stretched in front to keep her a prisoner. She was dressed in a gown which folk knew by John's description to have been her wedding-dress. He thought she said, "O Johnnie! what's sent you here?" to which he answered, "what keeps you here?" Katherine replied "I am well and happy but I can't get out, for I have eaten their food." Nisbet unfortunately did not know, or forgot to say, "Gude be aboot wis" (God bless us) – and Katherine was unable to give him a hint – so that, in a moment, the whole scene disappeared and she remained trapped in the hill.[14]

Once again, there would appear to be two possible explanations of the practice of taking human women to act as mothers. One is that the faeries had problems with child-bearing; the other, as also proposed before, is that faery women preferred to keep their figures and to enjoy their pleasure and, accordingly, were content for mortal girls to be brought in to act as 'brood mares.'

Mixed Race Children

As I have already indicated, there are plenty of folklore records of sexual relationships between fairies and humans. Inevitably, many of these unions will result in children; what do we know about these mixed-race families and their offspring?

Expert on fairy lore, Katharine Briggs, went as far as to write that the fairies "are apparently near enough in kind to mate with humans – closer in fact than a horse is to an ass, for many human families to claim fairy ancestry". Scottish expert J. F. Campbell said something very similar, observing that "mortals were separated from fairies by a very narrow line."[15]

---

14 Edmonston and Saxby, *The Home of a Naturalist*; *County Folk-Lore* vol. iii, 23–5.
15 Briggs, *The Fairies in Tradition and Literature,* 95; Campbell, *Popular Tales of the West Highlands,* vol.2, 76.

FAIRY BIRTHS

The veracity of these assertions is demonstrated by the singular example of the island of Guernsey, where the bulk of the population is of fairy descent. Once, a young girl went out to tend her families' cows. In the fields, she met a short but handsome stranger and they both fell for each other at once. He had come from Faery and they returned to his home together and lived there happily. His friends, however, were jealous of his new human wife, so they decided to go to Guernsey too to get themselves young and pretty partners. They emerged on the island at the cave of Les Creux des Faies and immediately engaged in battle with the local men, who fought to protect their womenfolk. The human males were defeated and only two survived, having hidden themselves in an oven. The fairies settled, married and had families but, after a period of time, had to return to Faery. They left behind a distinctive population of short, dark people and, to this day, any short islander is called "aën p'tit faitot" (a little fairy). Those locals who are tall and fair are descendants of the two human survivors.[16]

Mixed race families are entirely possible, then, and there seems neither doubt nor surprise about this in the folklore. When we learn about human-faery offspring, it is generally because there has been some problem in the relationship. Of course, our view of these matters is skewed, as we usually only hear about cases where partnerships went wrong – not those matches where the couple 'lived happily ever after.' Admitting that we only tend to see the failed matches, what can we say about fairy partnering and parenting? Probably the fairest

---

16   Marie de Garis, *Folklore of Guernsey,* 1975, Part V, 144.

THE FAERY LIFECYCLE

conclusion is that fairies are just as good, and as bad, as husbands, wives and parents as humans can be.

Andro Man of Aberdeen was tried for witchcraft in 1598. He disclosed to the court a decades-long relationship with the fairy queen. Over a period of thirty years, he said, he had enjoyed regular sexual contact with her and the couple had had "diverse bairnis" whom he'd since visited in *Elphame* (fairyland). These children were brought up by the mother, but at the same time Man was not entirely absent from their lives.

A reversal of this arrangement is seen with Katharine Jonesdochter of Shetland, tried for witchcraft in 1616. She confessed to a forty-year affair with a fairy man whom she called 'the bowman.' He first came to her when she was a teenager (a "young lass," as she described herself) and they had a child together. A relative recalled that she had seen "ane little creatour in hir awin hus amongst hir awin bairns quhom she callit the bowmanes bairn." In this case the child stayed with the (human) mother and the (fairy) father was seen once or twice a year – at Halloween and on Holy Cross Day (September 14th) – when he visited her for sex.

Both these cases seem to say more about gender roles in human and fairy society than they do about defaults or qualities of fairykind as mothers and fathers. There is, of course, no reason to assume that faery males are any less loving toward their spouses and children than females. All the same, an exception may have to be made for merfolk. The folklore record indicates that they are very often wanting in basic familial instincts and make very poor parents indeed. When in human form they appear as very handsome men, a fact of which they will take full advantage: they will come ashore to have sex with young girls and married women, but they very seldom linger to deal with the consequences (although there is one story of a merman who was forced to stay with his human family at Hilton of Cadboll in Easter Ross after a young girl managed to steal from him the magic belt that he used to swim underwater). In the ballad of the *Selkie of Sule Skerry,* the selkie father is rather more typical of his kind. He has first of all had his pleasure and made a woman pregnant before abandoning her; then he returns grudgingly upon hearing her complaints and gives her gold to 'buy' the child from her (what he calls a 'nurse-fee') – taking the boy away to raise him as a selkie in the sea.[17]

In many stories, a mermaid or selkie becomes a parent as the result of being captured by a human male on the shore. He has managed to find, and withhold from her, the seal skin or tail that she has shed temporarily, thereby preventing her from re-joining her people. The mermaid is forced to become her captor's wife and children inevitably follow over the succeeding years. Eventually, though, one of those infants comes across the seal skin hidden somewhere on the farm and mentions the discovery to the mother – who without hesitation leaves immediately to return to the sea and her own kind.

As can be seen, whether male or female, merfolk generally set a poor example as parents. The best that can be said for most mermaids is that they were akin

---

[17] W. T. Dennison, 'Orkney Folklore II: Selkie Folk,' *Scottish Antiquary,* vol.7, 1893, 175; F. Gordon-Cumming, *In the Hebrides,* 376.

to captives and unwilling partners, which may excuse a little their readiness to abandon their children. The few exceptions to this neglectful attitude to partners and offspring seem to arise where the human father is prepared to go to live with his wife beneath the waves.

The Welsh lake-maidens, the *gwragedd annwn,* also have a reputation for abandoning their husbands and families, although in these cases they would excuse themselves and blame the husbands for what happened. They are wooed in conventional manner by the human males and consent freely to marriage, but conditions or taboos are always imposed which – just as predictably – are violated in time by their husbands. These mothers are driven away from their families, therefore; they are not fleeing like the mermaids.

As we might expect, having fairy parents or ancestors does have some benefits for the children. John Rhys quotes in his *Celtic Folklore* from William Williams' 1802 book, *Observations on the Snowdon Mountains*, in which he discusses:

> "A race of people inhabiting the districts about the foot of Snowdon, were formerly distinguished and known by the nickname of *Pellings*, which is not yet extinct. There are several persons and even families who are reputed to be descended from these people…. These children and their descendants, they say, were called *Pellings*, a word corrupted from their [faery] mother's name, Penelope… there are still living several opulent and respectable people who are known to have

sprung from the *Pellings*. The best blood in my own veins is this fairy's."[18]

Rhys also mentions several times people living in the Pennant Valley in North Wales who are noted for their very good looks – flax yellow hair and pale blue eyes – which are said to be derived from a fairy ancestor called Bella.[19]

As well as physical charms, fairy parents can bestow significant gifts upon their part-human offspring. The faery wife of Llyn y Fan Fach was a typical Welsh 'lake maiden' who was driven off by her husband's violation of her taboos. Nonetheless, she kept in regular contact with her three sons, giving them each bags that are assumed to have contained medicinal herbs and teaching them marvellous healing skills, so that they became the famous physicians of Myddfai. Selkies could bestow great luck in fishing upon their half-human offspring by helping drive fish towards their nets. In a variant on this theme, one departed selkie mother daily left five fish on the shore for her young family to eat.[20]

In the Tudor *Ballad of Robin Goodfellow*, Robin is the son of Oberon, fathered upon a maid to whom he took a fancy. The father provides materially for his child's upbringing (although he is absent from the boy's life) and, when his son reaches his teens, Oberon comes to him and reveals his true nature and magical powers:

---

18 J. Rhys, *Celtic Folklore*, vol.1, 48, citing Williams 37–40.
19 Rhys, *Celtic Folklore*, vol.1, 96, 106, 108, 220 & 223; vol.2, 668.
20 A. Polson, *Our Highland Folklore Heritage*, 1926, 78 & 79.

> "King Oberon layes a scrole by him,
> that he might understand
> Whose sonne he was, and how hee'd grant
> whatever he did demand:
> To any forme that he did please
> himselfe he would translate;
> And how one day hee'd send for him
> to see his fairy state."

Finally, the offspring of matches with merfolk are generally readily identifiable by certain physical marks, all of which can be more or less disfiguring and problematic. The Kreenie family of Galloway was said to be descended from one of the merfolk and, as a result, all the women were bearded. The clan MacCodrum in the Hebrides had selkie ancestors and, as a result, lived as seals by day and as humans by night.[21]

There are accounts from the Scottish islands of children conceived between mermaids and human fathers who have webs between their fingers and toes. One such mother tried to trim these away but they regrew repeatedly until a horny crust developed – a feature that is still be seen amongst some island people today and which can limit the manual tasks they can undertake. On Shetland, a girl out gathering shell fish on the beach noticed that a seal was watching her from just off-shore. Thinking little more of it, she sat in a cave mouth to eat her lunch and fell asleep there. A few months later it became clear that she was pregnant and, when the child was born, it was revealed whom the parent was: the child

---

21 Trotter, *Galloway Gossip,* 182; MacGregor, *Peat Fire Flame,* 95.

FAIRY BIRTHS

had flippers, instead of hands, and was plainly the offspring of that seal. Fortunately for mother and baby, she dreamed that, if she went to a nearby inlet, she would find silver that would pay for her son's upbringing. Other versions of this story record that the child was either hairy all over and could not talk, but moaned like a seal, or had webbed fingers and toes that made walking very difficult.[22]

Mixed marriages with merfolk are most commonly mentioned, but faeries on land also have children with humans. The *fuaths* of Beann na Caltuinn in the Scottish Highlands intermarried with the local Munro family and, for generations afterwards, the children had manes and tails like their supernatural ancestors. Another version of the same story records that the *fuath* father refused to help the human mother look after their son, although he did agree to provide her with a daily supply of trout.[23]

The offspring of mixed parentage may well bear physical marks which clearly identify them as such. In light of this, it's worthwhile too considering what their status might be within the communities in which they live. So far as the faeries themselves are concerned, there may not be any prejudice towards part-human individuals. They actively steal human babies to supplement their population and kidnap adult women for sex. In fact, it's said that the faeries specifically want human children because they wish to raise a leader who will not fear iron blades and who will therefore be able to lead them in a

---

22 Nicolson, *Shetland Folklore*, 88; *www.tobarandualchais.co.uk*, 1954–56.
23 J. F. Campbell, *Popular Tales*, vol.2, 204–5; *Celtic Monthly*, vol.10, 1885, 211.

war to drive the mortals out of the land they have stolen from its previous, supernatural possessors.[24]

The position of half-faery infants in human society might not be so favourable. We do not have much information on this, but there is one Welsh story that suggests a rather negative attitude to such children. A fisherman in West Wales came across a mermaid in a sea cave and entered into a sexual relationship with her. They had a lot of children together, the text states, "*os gellid galw'r fath gynyrch ar y fath enw*" (if such a product can be called by such a name). In due course, the mother returned to visit her own people under the sea. Her children remained on land with their human family, but they were regularly teased about their heritage "*er hyn i gyd, yr oedd yr edliwiad mai Môrforwyn oeddei fam yn peri cryn drallod meddwl iddo*" (nevertheless, there was the accusation that he had a mermaid mother, which caused him considerable mental distress). It's evident from the tone of this that there was felt to be some shame (in Victorian Wales at least) in being the child of mixed parents.[25]

As a last comment on this matter, it will be seen that sexual intercourse and interbreeding with fairykind is both physically and biologically possible. Whether it is a wholly pleasurable experience is another question. The testimony of human men who have had relations with faery women always tends to suggest that the females are active and enthusiastic partners, being energetic and promiscuous. The experience for human women might not be so pleasant. Margaret Alexander of Livingston in 1647 confessed to a thirty-year affair with the fairy

---

24 B. Fairweather, *Folklore of Glencoe & North Lorn*, 1974, 2.
25 Glasynys, 'Yr Forforwyn,' in *Cymru Fu*, 1862, 434–444.

king. On one occasion, she recalled, he had lain with her upon the bridge at Linton, and, she claimed, his "natour" had been cold – in other words, during intercourse she found his penis to be icy inside her.[26] Margaret was being tried as a witch and, in other such interrogations, this sort of allegation was often made about the devil. For example, in 1645 Ellen Driver of Framlingham in Suffolk described to her accusers how the devil had "made carnal use of her," but that she had found him cold inside her. Sometimes it was not the devil's actual body that was felt to be cold but his semen. Given these antecedents, we need not perhaps take Margaret's claim about the faery king too seriously, as it may be a product more of the inquisitors' preconceptions imposed upon her during torture than a reflection of her actual experience.[27]

Faery Ointment

One last aspect of the faery new-born must be considered. As already mentioned, there are many stories concerning a human midwife or wet nurse who is called to assist with a faery birth and who is then asked to take care of the new-born baby, something which very often will include the task of regularly anointing it with a special ointment. The reason for doing this is never disclosed, but its purpose becomes apparent when the woman accidentally touches one of her own eyes with some of the salve and finds that she has acquired the second sight (in other words, that she can see faeries all the time).

---

26 See my *Love and Sex in Faeryland,* 2021; A. Macdonald, 'A Witchcraft Case of 1647,' *Scots Law Times,* April 10th 1937.
27 See too James VI/I, *Daemonologie,* 1597, 67.

The cream the midwife has to apply to the neonate clearly has a very important function. It seems that it has two properties. Firstly, it confers the faeries' magical powers upon the child: the ointment (or, sometimes, an oil) is most frequently applied to the eyes of the newborn – which implies that the power to see through faery illusion or invisibility is what is being conveyed – and also that faery babies are born with non-faery vision. Secondly, though, from time to time the treatment prescribed is to rub the baby all over with the substance (there are examples from Wales and Cornwall of this). This more general application seems to indicate that a more profound alteration of the child's physical nature is intended and that not just a power to penetrate concealment or disguise but a range of other magical abilities – to fly, to transform objects and the like – is being passed on.

It may also be that the ointment confers longevity or immortality and that, at birth, faery babies are much like human infants in terms of lifespan, so that they need some intervention to bestow a faery term of years upon them (I'll discuss faery immortality in detail later). There are a few brief mentions in verse and folklore of a faery practice of dipping changelings in order to liberate them from human mortality. Certainly, in the story of Eilean of Garth Dolwen it seems highly significant that the ointment has to be applied by the midwife to the half-human, half-faery child, perhaps to free it of its maternally inherited human frailties.

A further confirmation of the need to transform faery children with ointment comes from a Northumbrian story concerning the fostering of a faery child by a couple from Nether Whitton. They are required by the faery parents to anoint the child's eyes daily with a never-ending supply of ointment. Predictably, the tale ends unhappily with the man blinded for abusing the magic ointment and the boy taken back to Faery, but it seems clear that the treatment is something that has to be given to all faery infants, whoever their parents may be and wherever they're raised. The story also implies (yet again) that childcare may be too much trouble for faery parents. Note too that in June 1615 on Shetland, Janet Drever was scourged and banished by a church court when she admitted she had had carnal dealings and conversations with the fairies for twenty-six years, a relationship that culminated in her fostering a trow child in the hill of Westray.[28]

To conclude, it might have been imagined that magic qualities are inherent in faery-kind, central to their non-human nature, but it seems not. These attributes need to be specifically conveyed, failing which – presumably – the child would be little different to any other.

---

28   Grice *Folk Tales* c.1; *Maitland Club Miscellany,* vol.2, 167; R. M. Fergusson, *Rambling Sketches in the Far North,* 1883, 14.

CHAPTER TWO

Faery Childhood and Growth

By and large, we tend to assume that the faeries with whom people have encounters are adults and as a result we rarely give much thought to their growth, maturation or actual age. Nevertheless, a more careful reading of the sources reveals quite plentiful indications on these matters.

Fairy Children

Faery children are mentioned reasonably often in the folklore accounts, although humans only tend to come across them in less than happy circumstances. For example, a man out hunting on the Hebridean island of Barra saw what he thought was a sea otter eating a fish on a reef in Caolas Cumhan. However, when he raised his gun to his eye to shoot, he realised that he was actually looking at a mermaid mother holding her baby – so he spared the pair. In a second incident, a man came across a seal and her pup on the beach and caught the young one, aiming to strip it of its soft pelt. However, seeing the selkie mother's distress, he relented and released child, an act of mercy for which he was later rewarded in kind. In these two cases, the fae babies narrowly avoided death, but a number of infant mermaids have been seen for the very reason that they were dead. In 1810 two Manx merchildren were found on washed up rocks at the Calf of Man. Sadly, one of them had already expired but the other was saved – only to be displayed to the public in Douglas town.[29]

More often and puzzlingly, given how precious offspring must be, faery children seem to get lost. Most human encounters with fairy infants occur in cases where they have strayed or become separated from their parents. For instance, one evening on Shetland a man found a strange straw box in his farmyard. He put it in the house and went to feed his livestock and, when he returned inside, he heard an odd sound from inside the container, a little like "Foddle-dee-foodle-dee-doo," as well as the sound of feet kicking. A voice called out, asking to be released, and he realised there was a trow child inside. He promptly put the box outside again, hoping and assuming that the parents would return to collect their mislaid offspring. This response sounds a little neglectful, but his panic may be understandable. In fact, taking care of a lost youngster can be a canny, as well as a kind move: in another Shetland example, a little trow girl dressed in grey and brown was found lost by a family and was taken in for the night. She slept in the same bed as the human children and, the next morning, heard her mother calling her home and left quite contentedly. In recognition of this care, it appears, the children who had shared a bed with the girl grew up to be happy and prosperous.[30]

---
29 See my *Beyond Faery,* 2020, chapter 1.
30 Haldane Burgess, 'Some Shetland Folklore,' *Scottish Review,* vol.25, 1895, 96 & 100.

THE FAERY LIFECYCLE

Another faery girl was found lost and alone near Tower Hill, Middleton-in-Teesdale, in northern England. The woman who found her took the child home, sat her by the fire and gave her bread and cheese to eat, but the girl cried so bitterly that woman took pity on her distress and decided to return her to the place by the river where she'd been found. This was a spot where it was believed that the faeries came to bathe, so her hope was that the girl's parents would return for her – and several of stories indicate that they will do just that.[31]

Sometimes the faery infants are simply unlucky to encounter humans, as was the case with a fairy boy who was caught by two men hunting otters at Cwm Pennant in Gwynnedd in North Wales. They saw a red creature run and hide in the roots of a tree and managed to trap it in a sack. Pleased with their prize, the pair started to head home, but they heard a voice from the sack mournfully cry out 'My mother is calling me!' and were so shocked that they dropped their burden and ran off. Sometimes fairy children are just careless, as in the case of a pixie child captured near Zennor, in West Cornwall. A farmer was cutting furze when he spotted the young pixie asleep. He scooped it up and took it home, where it was named Bobby Griglans by the man's family. The child didn't seem too distressed by its situation and would play contentedly by the hearth with the family's children. One day, when all the youngsters had slipped outside to play, the pixie's parents appeared searching for him and he happily went home with them.[32]

---

31 Bord, *Fairies*, Appendix, 206; R. H. Horne, *The Elf of the Woodlands*.
32 Rhys, *Celtic Folklore*, 139; Bottrell, *Traditions*, vol.1, 74.

FAERY CHILDHOOD AND GROWTH

Perhaps Cornish pixie parents are especially careless. In Enys Tregarthen's 1940 story, *Skerry-Werry,* a widow living on Bodmin Moor hears a voice crying for her mother one evening. She goes out with a lantern to search and finds a tiny child alone in the heather. The widow cares for this little girl, who grows rapidly; at the same time, her presence seems to give the woman the gift of second sight. In another story from the same county, a farmer at Langreek, near Polperro, one evening found a miserable-looking human-like creature, sitting on a stone in the middle of a field. The tiny child was apparently very cold and hungry, so the farmer took him home to feed and warm him. The fairy boy seemed happy to stay and to play with the farmer's child but, after three or four days, a voice was heard in the farmyard, calling "Colman Grey!" At this the pixie boy sprang up, declared "My daddy is come," and flew out through the keyhole, never to be seen again.[33]

Another lost pixie child was discovered by a farmer living near Ottery St Mary in Devon. He was walking through his fields when he heard a voice crying out that he'd lost his 'Shilo.' Looking over a hedge, the farmer saw a little old man. Soon afterwards, he came across a tiny baby lying near one of his hay ricks and crying feebly. He took the child home to his wife, who revived it with bread soaked in warm cider. Realising that the baby must be the missing Shilo for whom the pixie had been searching, the man returned the infant to the spot where he'd found it. He then called out and quickly the old pixy appeared

---

[33] Tregarthen, *Folklore Tales,* 2020; Couch, *History of Polperro,* 134; *Choice Notes: Folk-Lore,* 73.

THE FAERY LIFECYCLE

and took back his child, without saying a word to the human. The couple feared they'd face punishment for removing the pixie baby, but instead they were rewarded with faery help and prosperity for the rest of their lives.[34]

On Shetland and Orkney, it was thought that, if a trow stayed out past dawn, she or he would find themselves 'day-bound,' and would be unable to return home under the hill until the next nightfall. This happened to a trow boy one time, who was later discovered by a crofter hiding in a peat cutting. The man felt sorry for the stranded child and took him home for shelter. The boy was given milk to drink, but he threw it up straight away and complained that the family were trying to poison him. This reaction is very odd given the great love fairy people generally show for dairy products; nevertheless, in this instance, the boy threatened to curse the household unless they let him go, which they had to do. In another version of this story, the boy apparently demanded heath and black bull's bladder to eat and then warned he would blow the house down unless he was released.[35]

Accidents will happen, of course, and in several of these cases the parents clearly searched extensively for the infant once they realised that it had got lost, indicating their concern for the child. There is also a little direct evidence of normal care and parenting by faery parents. For example, a fairy child fell ill and her mother approached a housewife living at Longhill, near Whithorn in southwest Scotland, asking for some milk

---

34 W. P. Merrick, 'Shilo – A Devonshire Folk Tale,' *Folklore*, vol.22, 1911, 48–49.
35 Nicolson, *Shetland Folklore*, 83; *www.tobarandualchais.co.uk*, 1955 & Dec.28th 1974.

for the poorly infant. Fairy children can get sick, just like human youngsters, and their families will naturally seek to take care of them – and they will reward any humans who take pity and assist. Faery care can extend to human infants too, demonstrating their natural parenting instincts. In an incident from South Uist, a human mother went to tend her animals, leaving a child alone at home. The boy got out of the house but was found by a fairy woman who took him back inside and comforted him by singing until his mother returned. The faery then warned the woman not to leave her child on his own again. This seems like friendly maternal advice, although it might possibly be a warning of the risk of abduction if there was any future neglect.[36]

The very same parental concern was shown by a selkie mother of half-human children. One of her boys was not very bright but was very strong. He found work in the local flour mill, but the miller used to mistreat the youth because of his learning disability. One day the mother appeared and sprayed the man with boiling hot water, badly scalding him in revenge for his abuse of her son.[37]

Infant Looks

What do these faery infants look like? On the whole, most of them are distinctly small and sound as if they are malnourished, although this could simply be a result of their wandering. Some are more memorable: the lost child found at Middleton in Teesdale had red eyes and

---
[36] Fraser, *Wigtown & Whithorn,* 355; *www.tobarandualchais.co.uk,* August 9th 1972 & January 24th 1960.
[37] Polson, *Our Highland Folklore Heritage,* 79.

the mermaid child on the Isle of Man was brown in colour except for violet scales on its tail and green coloured hair. In addition, there is some negative evidence to hand as well.[38]

It is a widespread belief that pretty, fair-haired and blue-eyed human babies are the most vulnerable to being snatched away by the fairies. For example, along the border between England and Wales it was said that "fine and solid" country babies were the ones preferred. In light of these popular beliefs, which were based on long experience, it might be proposed that the human infants taken were chosen precisely because they did *not* look like fairy offspring.[39]

Maturity

All the information available to us indicates that faery children grow up quite quickly. For instance, the accounts of them getting lost demonstrate that they are allowed considerable independence from an early age.

Sexual maturity apparently comes early in youth. For example, in the ballad *Leesom Brand*, which was mentioned in the last chapter, the hero falls in love with the daughter of the king of elf-land:

> "This ladye was scarce eleven years auld,
>   When on her love she was right bauld;
>   She was scarce up to my right knee,
>   When oft in bed wi' men I'm tauld."

---
38 Bord, *Fairies*, 206.
39 Simpson, *Welsh Border*, 73.

FAERY CHILDHOOD AND GROWTH

Within twelve months, or so of this, the girl was a mother. The boundaries of childhood, adolescence and adulthood are – in large measure – social constructions rather than biological categories and, in earlier British society, marriageability was expected at a much earlier age – especially as there was no formal education to occupy young people into their late teens or early twenties. This is reflected in the ballad, *The Elfin Knight,* which was first printed in 1674, but whose text is much older. The song involves a girl wishing that the fairy knight would come to her in her bed-chamber. He duly appears, but then complains that she is "over young a maid" to lie with any man, to which she replies "I have a sister younger than I, and she was married yesterday." Another version of the ballad is more precise, albeit reversing the age difference and removing any requirement for the couple to actually marry:

"I hae a sister eleven years auld,
 And she to the young men's bed has made bauld…
 And I mysell am only nine,
 And oh! sae fain, luve, as I woud be thine."

These ballads were composed in a rural, non-industrial society, the like of which faeries still inhabit, and seem to reflect the sexual and marriage practices of those communities.[40]

---

40 See my *Fairy Ballads,* 2020.

Older Faeries

A few words on faeries' later years are necessary to conclude this initial survey of the faery lifecycle. It is notable how often fairies are described as looking elderly (in human terms, anyway). For example, at Ramsey, on the Isle of Man, a little old man was sighted in 1912, who had white hair and a beard and very bright blue eyes. In another Manx example, two children were approached by two "withered hobgoblins, three feet high…" A pixie seen at Shaugh Bridge on Dartmoor, in 1897, was described as a little wrinkled and wizened man. The readiness of many modern witnesses to label the individuals they have seen as 'gnomes' or 'leprechauns' must in good measure derive from our images of these beings as elderly males. What people may be identifying as a particular class or species of faery may, in fact, simply be the older members of their community.[41]

Even so, we must set against these sightings the curious statement by Cornish author Enys Tregarthen that the *pobel vean* (the little people) of the south west showed their age by getting younger and fairer – or, at least, the fairy royalty did.[42]

---

[41] Gill, *Second Manx Scrapbook*, c.6; *Chambers Journal*, vol.24, 1855, 96; Coxhead, *Devon Traditions & Fairy Tales*, 49 & 51; see too *www.tobarandualchais.co.uk*, June 1957.
[42] Tregarthen, *The Pisky Purse*, 1905.

CHAPTER THREE

Faery Physique

As faeries grow and mature into adulthood, they take on the forms in which they are most commonly seen by human beings (although we must admit that some faeries, at least, are shapeshifters and may assume appearances quite unlike their innate and natural bodies). The variety of sizes and bodily shapes that can be encountered make definitive statements quite difficult. In this chapter, I shall discuss a range of key physical characteristics to try to determine what the 'typical' faery looks like. However, there are a couple of more general issues to address first.

One subject that I shall not attempt to tackle here is the ability of some faeries to transform into a variety of other forms. They can make themselves appear like a number of mammals or birds or a range of inanimate objects (some of which become alarmingly animate in order to terrify witnesses). Some faeries can even appear wholly formless, as shapeless lumps of jelly or wool. I have tackled these transformations and creatures comprehensively elsewhere and, accordingly, I will concentrate on anthropomorphic fairies in this book. For similar reasons, I will also exclude extensive discussion of the more or less human-like mermaids and the vast range of faery beasts that exist – which I have again focussed upon in another book.[43]

Corporeal Creatures?

> "Flesh and blood are what we are,
> Flesh and blood are who we are."[44]

The next matter to address is the continuing debate as to whether or not faeries have any solid, physical existence. These arguments have been made for several centuries and are still to be decisively resolved.

In his classic study, *The Secret Commonwealth of Elves, Fauns and Fairies,* Scottish Presbyterian minister Reverend Robert Kirk described the faeries as being in a "different State or Element." He defined this variously as "astral," with the fairies being possessed of "light, changable Bodies somewhat of the Nature of a condensed cloud" and "agitated as Wild-fire with Wind." Being composed of "congealed Air," this meant that they could not be physically wounded in the "fluid, active, aethereal Vehicles" which held them.[45]

Kirk was Scottish, and it is true that by the late nineteenth century the general Highland belief was that the *sith* folk were not flesh and blood but spirits who looked like men and women, albeit smaller in stature.[46] They had no solidity and a hand could pass straight through them, as if through a ghost. The same belief prevailed in Wales:

---
43 See my *Faery,* 2020, c.4 and *Beyond Faery,* 2020, especially c.9.
44 From 'Persons Unknown' by the *Poison Girls,* 1981.
45 Sections 1, 3 & 7.
46 see Evans Wentz *Fairy Faith* 102, 104, 105, 109 & 114.

the popular conception was that the fairies didn't have physical bodies and so could not be caught. They lived in a materially different sort of world which would change any human who visited it.[47] One Welsh account depicts the faes dancing on the tips of rushes, evidently being both tiny and insubstantial. Commenting on this report at the very end of the Victorian era, Professor John Rhys remarked that "Though it used to be said that they were spiritual and immortal beings, still they ate and drank like human beings; they married and had children."[48] Modern reports still contain elements suggestive of the faeries' non-material nature: a number of recent witnesses have described them passing through solid objects, people as well as walls, as if they were not there.[49]

Given these persistent ideas, it is strange then that it is simultaneously accepted that ordinary mortals can have physical contact with fairies – dancing with them, nursing their babies and, indeed, fathering babies upon them (as we have already seen).

Generally, therefore, the practical manifestations or expressions of popular belief assume that faery folk are as real and tangible as we are: they can jostle and pinch humans, they can fire projectiles at us; in other words, faery is a parallel or neighbouring world that is just as corporeal as our own.

Various witnesses attest convincingly to the tangibility of fairies. A girl from Kent met a faery man leading a horse in her garden. He put his hand on her wrist "and his

---
[47] Wentz, *Fairy Faith,* 138, 140 & 144–145.
[48] Rhys, *Celtic Folklore,* 83; this is found too in the broadsheet ballad the *Fairies Fegaries*, so it is clearly a traditional concept.
[49] Johnson, *Seeing Fairies,* 94, 182, 185, 187, 190, 260 & 298.

touch was cool, not cold like a fish or a lizard but much cooler than a human touch." Especially persuasive is an account from the Isle of Man. A woman from Ballasalla told George Waldron how her ten-year-old daughter had met a large crowd of little people up on the mountains. Some had tried to abduct her, others had objected to this and tried to protect her and, as a result, the faeries had fallen to fighting amongst themselves. Some of the fairies then spanked the girl for causing the dissension. When she got home, she had distinct prints of tiny hands on her buttocks and, when her family went to the spot where she said she'd been assaulted, they found spots of blood on the ground.[50]

As the last example shows, faeries can be hurt exactly as we can. The Reverend Kirk admitted that: "These Subterraneans have Controversies, Doubts, Disputes, Feuds and Sidings of Parties" just like humans and these conflicts lead, just as they do with us, to "Fighting, Gashes, Wounds and Burialls..." I will discuss fairy fatalities later and will focus here on their susceptibility to injury. A good example of this is found in the story of 'Big Kennedy' of Lianachan, near Lochaber. A *glaistig* had been causing terror and death in the neighbourhood and Kennedy managed to catch the creature and lock her in his barn. He then forced her to swear on a plough share that she would never molest the local people again. However, Kennedy had heated up the coulter in the fire. When the *glaistig* touched it, she was burned to the bone. She leaped out of the window with a screech and then

---

[50] Johnson, *Seeing Fairies*, 2014, 55; Waldron, *A Description of the Isle of Man*, 1731.

"put out three bursts of the blood of her heart" whilst cursing the man.[51]

It's also worth noting that fairies will steal human food, and human livestock, from which it follows that they must eat the same things as us. Again, some authorities (such as the Reverend Kirk) have said that the faeries subsist by extracting the nutritious essence of the foodstuffs – called the *foison* in English and the *toradh* in Gaelic – leaving behind the substance, albeit devoid of its nutritional benefit. Kirk described elves "feeding on the Pith or Quintessence of what the Man eats…" deriving nourishment from what he called "aetheriall Essences." He even went so far as to suggest that some of the *sith* folk exist "by only sucking into some fine spiritous liquors, that pierce lyke pure Air and Oyl" and compared to which the even foison is "more gross."[52]

These theories notwithstanding, there is also plentiful evidence that the fairies eat the actual substance itself. For example, one Dartmoor farmer, on two successive mornings, found ash and embers in his hearth and one of his cows reduced to skin and bones. On the third night he resolved to keep watch. Just as he had suspected, some pixies appeared and dragged the cow into the kitchen, where they proceeded to kill, flay and roast it. After their feast, however, they reassembled the beast from its hide and bones. A related idea in the Scottish Highlands was that when a cow fell off a cliff, the only way to stop the fays stealing the carcase was to act quickly and put a nail

---

51 Kirk, *Secret Commonwealth,* chapter 11; Carmichael, *Carmina Gadelica,* vol.2, 302–3– see too J. Rhys, *Folklore,* vol.3, 375.
52 Kirk, *Secret Commonwealth,* cc.1 & 3 and Conclusion, Question 3.

THE FAERY LIFECYCLE

in it, the iron acting as a defence against supernatural interference.[53]

Equally, the Welsh faes, the *tylwyth teg*, keep their own cattle, which are generally known as the *gwartheg yr llyn* (lake cattle). Often these beasts emerge from the lakes and, rather like their owners, can interbreed with mortal kind, profitably improving the quality of the humans' cows' milk and flesh. The *tylwyth teg* surely have no need of physical beasts if they aren't consuming their physical flesh and milk. Similar stories are known in Scotland – where crofters are able to benefit from herds of *crodh sith* (fairy cattle).[54]

On this same theme, a further demonstration of the compatibility of human and fairy food is found is the story of a faery cow given to humans in a time of famine and drought. The faery queen took pity on the sufferings of the locals and provided a cow with a never-ending supply of milk – so long as each household took just one pail full each day. The gift was eventually abused and lost, but the key point for us is that the fairy cow's milk could be consumed safely by the people. Another illustration of the same principle comes from the Scottish Borders. An old woman called Nanzy had long been on very good terms with the local fairies. They would often give her rolls of faery butter, which she would not only eat herself but would sell at market, making clear its comestibility.[55]

---

[53] J. Coxhead, *Devon Traditions & Fairy Tales*, 51; MacGregor, *Peat Fire Flame* 3.
[54] Rhys, *Celtic Folklore*, 10, 144 & 149; McPherson, *Barra*, 188.
[55] *Bye Gones*, July 1893, 118–119; Burne, *Shropshire Folklore*, 39–40; Anon, *Notes & Anecdotes Illustrative of the Incidents, Characters & Scenery Described in the Novels of Sir Walter Scott*, 1833, 200.

FAERY PHYSIQUE

As a last, gruesome, demonstration of the very physical nature of faery food, I will cite two examples from the Scottish Highlands. Firstly, the supernatural water horses called the *each uisge* and the kelpie will both carry off, drown and consume human beings. Often, the only trace of the hapless victim that can be found is their entrails, that float ashore later – proof positive that they have been devoured whole.[56] Secondly, there is a species of vampire-like creature, called the *glaistig*, that will seduce unsuspecting men and then drain them of their blood. The hag called the *baobhan sith* is similarly anthropophagous.[57]

All in all, then, faeries are as solid and real as we are. As one writer expressed it in 1846, the faery folk "partake of the nature of men, and have the power of multiplying their species, and also of rendering themselves invisible, though endowed with material bodies." There might conceivably be some distinction between the physical nature of the human sized and smaller fairies. Maybe, too, there are regional differences or simply some inconsistency in our understanding, but most of the evidence indicates that their bodies are very much like our own, albeit endowed with magical powers to disappear, fly through the air and to change shape.[58]

---

56 See my *Beyond Faery;* see too Sutherland, *Folklore Gleanings,* 98; Mary McCulloch, 'Folklore of the Isle of Skye,' *Folklore,* vol.33, 1922, 307; Grant, *Myth, Tradition,* 2; Nicholson, *Golspie,* 17 & 21; MacGregor, *Peat Fire Flame,* 72 & 77.
57 MacDougall & Calder, *Folk Tales,* 243 & 259; *Celtic Monthly,* vol.3, 1894, 176; 'Faery tales'" in *Celtic Review,* vol.5, 164.
58 'Manners, Traditions & Superstitions of the Shetlanders,' *Fraser's Magazine,* vol.34, 1846, 485.

Weight

The weight of fairies will, of course, reflect both their substance and their size. Scottish faery-lore expert John Francis Campbell claimed in 1862 that Manx fairies have neither bodes nor bones. They are partly human and partly spiritual in their nature, he said, and are visible to men only when they choose. It's not clear what Campbell's source was for this statement; most Manx witnesses don't seem to doubt the corporeality of the faeries they have seen, although they do often acknowledge that they may be less robust or solid than us. For instance, one writer described them as small and delicate, looking handsome from a distance but up close being revealed as decrepit and withered. Another witness felt them walk on her and said they were "as light as cats." A further witness confirmed that they were "very little and very light," yet by way of contrast, a certain Mr Collister saw them once playing in the parlour of his house and described then as "lumps of boys" which surely implies that, whilst they may not have been very tall, they were solid enough. [59]

A few modern witnesses have commented upon the apparent weightlessness of the faeries they saw. Most striking is the testimony of painter John Duncan, who saw two members of the *sith* on Iona. They were both tall, yet "their feet did not bend the tall heather over which they walked." In many reports, the want of weight may be ascribed to the fairies' tiny size, but here it

---

59 Campbell, *Popular Tales of the West Highlands*, vol.1, 81, A. Moore, *Folklore of the Isle of Man*, c.3; *Yn Lioar Manninagh*, III; Roeder, *Manx Folktales*, 11.

suggests an overall insubstantiality which relates back to the previous section.[60]

Height

Of all the aspects of faery anatomy, there seems to be the greatest disagreement about their stature. As we shall discover, a very wide range of heights has been reported, and explaining these disparities confronts us with a significant problem. One approach is to postulate different 'tribes' or races of faeries within the overall fae population. Welsh writer David Jenkins did this when describing the fairies of Snowdon: he distinguished small fairies living amidst the bracken and heather of the mountains and larger beings who resided near human farms, from which they stole dairy products. Another explanation is to propose that all apparent variations are merely the result of faery magic and are perceptual rather than real.[61]

The Exmoor pixies have been compared in height to "little children."[62] Those of Dartmoor have been portrayed as extremely tiny creatures – much smaller than children – who can get into flower bells and "many other places where girls and boys cannot creep." Nevertheless, they can change their size, so that the pixies have also been estimated as being eighteen inches tall on average, although heights ranging from twelve inches to three feet have been reported. Because of their small size,

---

60 Johnson, *Seeing Fairies*, 57, 174 & 228.
61 D. E. Jenkins, *Bedd Gelert: Its Facts, Fairies & Folklore*, 1899, 153.
62 Snell, *Book of Exmoor*, 1903, 255.

they're often said to look like dolls.[63] This comparison of faery-kind to dolls is one that seems to have been made with increasing frequency in modern sightings, simply perhaps because of the mass market for Barbies and the like.[64]

In Cornwall, an old woman who came across a Halloween pixie fair at Pendeen saw a small but handsome crowd assembled: "none more than two feet high, and rather slender in make…" Fairies seen in a field near St Buryan were said to be about a yard (one metre) tall; a group spotted in 1830, crossing the road into the churchyard of St Kea, were estimated to have been eighteen inches in height. In the early 1870s some small people, about one and a half feet tall, were seen coming out of a hole in the cliffs at Mousehole. Elsewhere in the county, it was said in mid-Victorian times that the pixies were about "the height of a candlestick" whilst those seen around Polperro were described as being a 'span' (about nine inches) in height. Some pixies spotted dancing near Land's End were likened, rather imprecisely, to little children. Interestingly, in Cornish tradition the fairies' exercise of their shape-shifting power has a serious side effect: each time they resume their normal appearance they get smaller, so that over time they dwindle away

---

63 A. Bray, *Peeps on Pixies*, 1854, 11; Page, *An Exploration of Dartmoor*, 1895, 39; W. Bottrell, *Traditions and Hearthside Stories*, 1870, vol.1, 77; J. Coxhead, *Devon Traditions & Fairy Tales*, 1959, 49; G. Herbert, 'Devonian Folklore,' *Devonshire Association for the Advancement of Science*, vol.2, 1867, 80; *Choice Notes & Queries*, 1859, 26; K. Roberts, *Folklore of Yorkshire*, 63.
64 Johnson, *Seeing Fairies*, 66, 83, 93, 124, 152, 193 & 231; *Fairy Census*, no.33, 146, 263 & 377.

until they reach the size of ants and are, essentially, lost.[65]

On the Isle of Man, the fairies are called '*yn mooinjer veggey*,' the little people, and sightings have described a range of diminutive sizes, from very tiny up to the height of an infant of seven or eight. At the bottom end of the range was one fairy sighted in a road by two boys who was five to six inches tall.[66] In contrast, John Davies, a herb doctor of Ballasalla, recorded in 1910 that he had "seen some who were about two and a half feet high and some who were as big as we are." Interestingly, too, the Manx faeries have been said not to be as small as those in England are – or at least, have come to be perceived.[67]

Whilst numerous accounts agree that the Manx little people are indeed small, the comparison most often made is to children: two men from Sulby were walking home late one night when they saw twelve to fourteen little people run across the road just ahead of them. Despite their height, the pair didn't think these beings could have been children as it was so late and because they could find no trace of them where they'd just crossed the highway. The men concluded they must have been fairies. Similarly, in 1888, a man out shooting in a wood spotted two little figures peering at him from behind a tree. At first, he thought they must be the children of the woodsman, but they were very small and clothed in brown, so he

---

65 'Common Antiquities & Folklore of Cornwall,' *Royal Cornwall Gazette*, December 19th 1879, 6; Bottrell, *Traditions & Hearthside Stories*, vol.2, 73, 161, 162 & 245 Couch, 'Cornish Folklore,' *Penzance Natural History & Antiquarian Society Report*, in *Royal Cornwall Gazette*, Nov.11th, 1853, 6; J. Couch, *History of Polperro*, 134; Wentz, *Fairy Faith*, 142, 155 & 181.
66 *Manx Notes & Queries*, 1904, 117.
67 Evans Wentz, *Fairy Faith*, 123; Robertson, *A Tour*, 76; Mona Douglas, 'Secret Land of Legends,' *The Times*, Jan.2nd 1970, 27.

concluded that they had to be fairies. Crowds of fairies seen near Ballasalla were also described as being "like little boys." Some other fairies, observed walking along the top of a wall at Ballaugh, were estimated to have been about two feet high. Manx folklorist Dora Broome, meanwhile, described the *mooinjer veggey* as being "just the height of a man's elbow."[68]

All of these reports notwithstanding, not all of the Manx fairies seem to be tiny: some look to us like adults. An Edwardian witness, a Mr J. H. Kelly, described how he had once met "four figures as real to look upon as human beings, and of medium size, though I am certain they were not human." We should again remind ourselves that such differences in size need not indicate different types of faery. The faeries wield magical powers and they can appear to us to be small – but they can just as easily make themselves big, if and when they want to.[69]

The *tylwyth teg* in Wales are, by and large, described as small – if not miniscule: for instance, fairies regularly seen dancing at Corwrion did so to the light provided by a single glow-worm. Another witness, at Cwm Silyn in Eryri (Snowdonia), saw "a large crowd of people, or things in the shape of people, about a foot in stature." The *tylwyth teg* have been compared to men and women in their appearance and behaviour – yet having the stature of six-year-old children. In the early eighteenth century, Polly Williams from Trefethin in Monmouthshire used to meet with some *tylwyth teg* dancing as she was travelling to or from school. Initially she approached them because

---

[68] Gill, *Second Manx Scrapbook*, c.6; Broome, *More Fairy Tales*, 10.
[69] Gill, *Manx Scrapbook*, c.4 'German;' Wentz, *Fairy Faith*, 134; Roeder, *Manx Folktales*, 3; Broome, *Fairy Tales*, 106.

she thought that they were children as well, but she soon saw by their mature faces that they were much older than her.[70] The "throng of dwarfish people" seen in 1910 by the nurse from Rhosmynydd Nursing Committee (see earlier) were said to have been the height of children aged eight or ten, with brown withered faces and hands like tiny claws. The Welsh mine faeries, the *coblynau*, have been characterised as "about half a yard in height and very ugly to look upon." Oddest of all is the account of a crowd of little creatures seen in Glynllifon Park near Pwllheli in about 1870, which were described as being "the size of guinea pigs and covered with red and white spots."[71]

Turning to Scotland, folklore expert John Gregorson Campbell declared that "the true belief is that the fairies are a small race, the men about 'four feet or so' in height and the women, in many cases, not taller than a little girl (*cnapach caileig*)." Even so, Campbell also recognised that there was a variety in heights, from small beings for whom a single potato would be a burden up those of human stature. Islay tradition mentions a brownie called the Black Elf who was "the eighth part measure of a carl [man]." A Barra crofter called Domhull Dubh, who decided to plough on St Brendan's Day, was punished for his impiety by the saint. He sent a magic mist which shrank Domhull to "a mere mannikin, no bigger than a

---

70 Rhys, *Celtic Folklore*, 60, 111, 152, 158 & 222; Robin Gwyndaf, *Fairylore: Memorates and Legends from Welsh Oral Tradition*, in Narvaez, *Good People*; Sikes, *British Goblins*, 82; Jones, *The Appearance of Evil Apparitions*, no.117.
71 Dorothea Pugh Jones, 'A Case Not Entered,' *Welsh Outlook*, vol.18(2), February 1931, 45; Wirt Sikes, *British Golains*, 24; Rhys, *Celtic Folklore*, 220.

THE FAERY LIFECYCLE

dwarf." The sinner still wasn't discouraged, though, and tried to carry on with his work, in response to which a second mist descended, shrinking him so that he was "no bigger than a fairy man of the knoll." This, plainly, is significantly smaller than a dwarf. More recently recorded reports reiterate and reinforce these statements: some fairies seen at Cuilken in Sutherland were "just like ordinary people, but not half the size" whereas a crowd of up to two hundred sighted at Reay in Caithness were "about the size of bottles."[72]

Further north still, the trows of Orkney and Shetland are also described as small – no more than a metre tall – and very ugly; one witness said they were "no bigger than big bottles." The lowland Scottish faeries living under hillocks have been said to be child-sized – although one source also described them vividly (if unhelpfully) as being no larger than a bottle. The faery man of the ballad, *The Wee Wee Man*, has legs only six inches long. Yet again, these diminutive fays can be found alongside fays who are just the same in height and form as adult humans.[73]

As a final illustration, in June 1916 it was reported that a Mr Massey Taylor had been visiting Kew Gardens when he saw some fairies. Sitting in front of the palm

---

[72] Campbell, *Superstitions of the Highlands & Islands*, 1900, 10; Macgregor, *Peat Fire Flame*, 52; Carmichael, *Carmina Gadelica*, vol.2, 233; *www.tobarandualchais.co.uk*, May 31st 1983 & July 1955.

[73] Alan Bruford, *Trolls, Hillfolk, Finns and Picts*, in Narvaez, *Good People*; Aitken, *Forgotten Heritage* 1; *www.tobarandualchais. co.uk*, Dec.18th 1972; Margaret Bennett, *Balquhidder revisited*, in Narvaez, *Good People*; J. Campbell, *Waifs & Strays of Celtic Tradition*, 1895, vol.5, 86; for the *Wee Wee Man*, see my *Fairy Ballads*, 2020.

house, he had looked across the adjacent pond to a glade beyond and had seen groups of little beings, about eighteen inches high, dancing in circles or chasing each other on the far shore. Despite their animation and playfulness, he observed, they did not resemble children, but rather "little quaint old people, with mature minds, who still retained the sprightliness of youth."[74]

We could accumulate examples almost endlessly, but those already give a very good idea of the general content of the folklore record. What emerges seems to be a fairly marked distinction between those fairies who are of normal human height and those that are noticeably smaller. The *gwragedd annwn*, the Welsh lake-women, the mermaids, selkies, Green Ladies, hags, banshees, *lhiannan shees, leannan sith* and various other examples are all of human stature. Moreover, many of these females end up in sexual relationships and marriages with human males, from which it seems reasonable to assume that they are of a similar height to their lovers – or at least of the stature of more mature adolescents. Indeed, the elf-maiden kidnapped by Wild Edric after he saw her dancing in the Clun Forest in Shropshire was described as being "taller and larger than women of the human race." Assuming that the original Latin chronicler was not indulging in wholly unnecessary tautology when he described these fairies, we do seem to be told something about their build, here, as well as their height.[75]

---

74 'Fairies at Play,' *Cambrian Daily Leader,* June 15th 1916, 1.
75 Burne & Jackson, *Shropshire Folklore,* 59–61; Walter Map, *De Nugis Curialum,* Part II: the Latin text describes the faes as "*majoresque nostris et proceriores.*"

These instances aside, the rest of the faery race are consistently described, to some degree or other, as significantly smaller than adult humans. We have seen some of the comparisons made: to children of different ages, to pygmies, to apes and to smaller creatures, or to dolls and other inanimate objects of similar dimensions.[76]

To try to give more precision to this catalogue, I analysed the reports of sightings to be found in the recent *Fairy Census,* in Marjorie Johnson's *Seeing Fairies* and in a number of other twentieth century books on the subject, such as Janet Bord's *Fairies.* The combined records of estimated height from all these sources indicate that a little over half of the faeries sighted are under one foot or thirty centimetres in height. Around a fifth are over one yard or one metre tall, leaving about a quarter falling between those two limits. Even allowing for the fact that preconceptions about fairy size may unconsciously bias individuals towards *under*estimating their stature, as well as there being a likely tendency *not* to remark upon cases where the fairies are of human height, it is clear that the majority of the British faery population are, indeed, quite small.[77]

Strength

William Howells, describing the *tylwyth teg* in 1831 observed that the faeries were "always denoted to be puny beings, although, by the bye, it does not appear they were by their numerous and efficient actions."

---

[76] See my *Fayerie,* 2019.
[77] Johnson, *Seeing Fairies,* 2014; Bord, *Fairies – Real Encounters with Little People,* 1997.

FAERY PHYSIQUE

This predisposition to think of little faes as being weak persists still.[78]

The build of faeries is usually unremarkable, although some modern sightings have included a number of cases where the spindly or gangly nature of the being was especially noticeable. For example, some lanky figures over six feet tall were seen near Galashiels early in the twentieth century;[79] in the much more recent *Fairy Census* we find similar reports, such as a "very tall and very skinny" tree spirit with a spear seen in Sussex during the early 2010s.[80]

It's very apparent that there is great variation in body form between different types or classes of faery and, as might be anticipated, strength tends to be a factor of size. Some of the bulkier individuals, for example the boggarts and hobgoblins, are also memorable for their brawn *and* endurance. It's said that a single hob can do the work of ten men in half the time it would take them; one was strong enough to raise a cart above its head on to a roof (as a prank) whilst another lifted a fully loaded wagon when its wheel got trapped. They regularly carry large stones with ease. A hob on a farm in Furness strived so hard one night that he worked the farmer's horse to death. The Scottish *gruagach* is renowned for its immense strength whilst the Manx *fynoderee* will, like its English counterparts, perform great feats of farm work; at the same time, it has the strength to crush a plough share like putty with its hand. Kelpies, in human form, can tear oak trees out of the earth; similarly, in the ballad *Hynde*

---

[78] Howells, *Cambrian Superstitions*, 110.
[79] Johnson, *Seeing Fairies*, 84–85;
[80] *Fairy Census*, 2014, no.70, 97, 129, 147 & 181.

Etin the faery hero is able to pull up the tallest tree in the wood by its roots.[81]

The majority of the faeries do not have this superior strength, but they make up for this deficiency in stamina and cooperation. The best examples of these qualities are the stories from across Britain that involve faeries objecting to the site chosen by humans to construct a new church. In these accounts, the building materials – masonry blocks, timber, tools and the rest – are repeatedly moved overnight to another location, until the builders finally take the hint and accept the new site allocated to them. The stones for the new St Chad's at Rochdale were moved twice; those for Castel church on Guernsey three times and those for the new church at Stowe near Daventry a record nine times.[82] Only rarely (and very puzzlingly) is magic deployed to move the stonework; more often the faeries simply form a chain and laboriously pass the blocks hand to hand – through communal endeavour accomplishing what individual muscle power could not have managed.[83]

---

81   See my *Beyond Faery*, 132–134, 141 & 148; I. Barton, *North Yorkshire Folk Tales*, 2014, 85; J. Atkinson, *Forty Years in a Moorland Parish*, 1891, 65; 'Correspondence,' *Folklore* vol.8, 69; Bowker, *Goblin Tales*, 247; Douglas, *Scottish Faery and Folk Tales*, 200.
82   Harland, *Lancashire Legends*, 53; MacCulloch, *Guernsey Folklore*, 1903, 221; T. Sternberg, *Dialect & Folklore of Northamptonshire*, 1851, 139.
83   Elder, *Tales & Legends of the Isle of Wight*, 220; R. Chambers, *Popular Rhymes of Scotland*, 1870 edition, 80; A. Small. *Antiquities of Fife*, 1823, 152–3; Groome, *Ordnance Gazetteer of Scotland*, 1882, vol.1, 287; J. Cargill Guthrie, *Vale of Strathmore*, 1875, 35.

Motion

The anthropomorphic fairies are bipedal, just like humans, and they walk with an upright gait. This fundamental and obvious fact is best evidenced by reference to the faeries' dancing. Keen as they are on this pastime, it does not appear that their preferred dance steps are anything more than skipping in circles.

The reason this simple detail of faery motion can often be overlooked is because the faeries have so many other, more exotic ways, of getting around. They can fly on ragwort stems; they may travel inside whirlwinds; they keep horses (and sometimes other beasts such as donkeys and cats) for riding;[84] from time to time, they have been observed floating through the air, occasionally in quite a sinuous fashion; they might simply appear and disappear.[85]

All the same, this variety of forms and means of locomotion should not obscure from us the fact of the faeries' basic ability to get about on two feet nor the fact that they are often seen in procession or walking alone.

Hair

Faery hair is frequently remarked upon, most commonly for its beauty. The details revealed by the recorded sightings are, nonetheless, surprising. The Somerset fairies are described as being red-haired.[86] As a rule, the

---
84 *Y Cymmrodor,* vol.7, 1886, 115, 'Anglesey Folklore;' W. Wilson, *Folklore of Uppermost Nithsdale,* 1904, 99.
85 E. Jones, *The Appearance of Evil Apparitions,* 2003, 59.
86 Tongue, *Somerset Folklore,* 1965, 113.

Manx fairies have red hair too and (it is reported) they prefer to abduct red-headed humans.[87]

The Welsh *tylwyth teg* have been described as having lovely white skin, which is combined with red hair or sometimes, much more alarmingly, with white hair and white eyes. A story dated to 1903 from the Welsh borders substantiates this. An old woman living at Trellech, near Monmouth, described the fairies as being fairly small with "queer complexions." They were the size of a six-year-old child, barefoot, dressed in white with lovely white skin, but they had white hair and white eyes as well. From some earlier date in Victorian times there comes the story of John Jones, a farm labourer of Perthrhys farm near Aberystwyth. Walking home across Rhosrhydd Moor one moonlit night, John realised two boys were following him. Although it was late, he at first assumed they were just local youths messing around. However, the boys then left the roadway and started to dance in an "unearthly" manner, at which point Jones realised that they were both "perfectly white."[88]

The fairly common hymns of praise to the loveliness of fairy hair aren't the whole story, we must therefore acknowledge. Shakespeare, in his 1593 poem, *Venus and Adonis*, made an interesting reference to faeries' locks:

> "Bid me discourse, I will enchant thine ear,
> Or like a fairy trip upon the green,
> Or, like a nymph, with long dishevell'd hair,
> Dance on the sands, and yet no footing seen."

---
87 Gill, *Second Manx Scrapbook*, c.6.
88 J. Simpson, *Folklore of the Welsh Border*, 1976, 73; J. C. Davies, *Folklore of West and Mid Wales*, 1911, 124.

FAERY PHYSIQUE

Nearly two hundred years later, we hear the same phrase again. In 1792 an account of the parish of Liberton in Edinburgh described the local fairy women as being "girls of diminutive size, dressed in green with dishevelled hair, who frequented sequestered places and at certain times conversed with men." Evidently those men weren't put off by the state of their hair. A contemporary report from Kirkmichael in Banffshire described fairy women appearing to travellers, "with dishevelled hair floating over their shoulders and with faces more blooming than the vermeil blush of a summer morning." A little later, another Scottish witness portrayed young fairy women as "beautiful young girls, clad in green, with loose dishevelled hair, who frequent woods and valleys. Men have often seen and spoken to them." Perhaps part of the attraction for those human males was indeed the fresh, natural look of the faes, their unkemptness being suggestive of a wild or uninhibited nature that contrasted alluringly with that of the well-groomed (and well chaperoned) girls of their everyday acquaintance.[89]

A wider consideration of faery descriptions indicates that the state of the hair does indeed serve to signal the character and attractiveness of the being as a whole. The brownies and the less friendly goblins and hags almost always seem to be described as having shaggy, coarse, dark hair. For human witnesses, in fact, it's almost impossible to conceive of a malign entity that, at the same time, has sleek, groomed locks; our minds unconsciously reject such a pairing. Nonetheless, some modern witnesses

---

[89] Rev. Thomas Whyte, *An Account of the Parish of Liberton in Mid-Lothian,* 1792; *Statistical Account of Scotland,* vol.12, 462; Shaw, *History of the Province of Moray,* 1827, 287.

have described seeing faes with feathers growing in their hair (or even with feathers *instead* of hair). Perhaps these reports make sense of a description of the Welsh *tylwyth teg* as "dressed all in white, with something like feathers waving in the wind."[90]

We must turn now to consider mermaids, creatures who traditionally have been renowned for their masses of long hair (if only to preserve their womanly modesty). In fact, sightings of mermaids have described them variously as having short dark hair, flowing red locks, coarse hair, curly but oily green hair, and (most often) that luxurious fair hair in which they take such great pride, sitting for hours on rocks combing it and admiring themselves in mirrors. Legend aside, a salutary report comes from Orkney. A man developed a passion for a mermaid he saw combing her hair on a rock off shore. He followed her to a cavern, but up close discovered that she was nowhere near as bonny as he had imagined: she had seaweed for hair, ugly scales and a mouth like a shark's. He fled.[91]

The lovely blonde mermaid in the sea is a cliché, but she's not alone. In Scottish rivers lives the *ceasg*, a creature of great beauty (once you have reconciled yourself to the fact that she is half woman and half salmon). Her hair has been described as being "long and flossy," which I understand to mean that it is very pale and silky: the name itself signifies a tuft of wool, linen or silk.

All in all, then, the fairies' hair is distinctive and

---

90 see John Dathen, *Somerset Fairies and Pixies*, 30; Howells, *Cambrian Superstitions*, 112.
91 *www.tobarandualchais.co.uk*, March 17th 1979; see too my *Beyond Faery*, c.1.

noticeable although, in fact, it is not always one of their most alluring qualities for humans.

Skin

Both the texture and tone of faery skin need to be considered. One Cornish witness described male pixies as "swarthy in complexion, [whereas] the women had a clear complexion of peach-like bloom. None ever appeared to be more than five and twenty to thirty years old." Another Cornish account described how:

> "The [pixie] men were much darker complexioned than the women, yet they were all very good looking, with sparkling dark eyes, well-shaped noses, sweet little mouths, and dimpled cheeks and chins. Not one among them, that she saw, had a spotty face or purple-top nose, because they drink nothing stronger than honey-dew. Some, to be sure, appeared to be rather aged, yet all were sprightly, merry, and gay."[92]

Mermaids too have been credited with a "plump round face, blue eyes and rosy cheeks." Despite their outdoor life, exposed to the elements, all of these supernaturals seem to be fresh and healthy rather than weather-beaten.[93]

It is also very important to highlight the fact that Faery tends to be conceived of as a very white, very Western

---
92 Wentz, *Fairy Faith,* 177; Bottrell, *Traditions & Hearthside Stories,* vol.2, 161.
93 Polson, *Our Highland Folklore Heritage,* 74.

THE FAERY LIFECYCLE

European community. Today, only a few writers envisage non-white fairies – but this has not always been the case. For example, in Shakespeare's *Midsummer Night's Dream* the fairy court has connections with the far east, with Titania and Oberon disputing over a boy "stolen from an Indian king" whose mother served as a "votaress" to Titania, the pair having been in the habit of sitting together gossiping in the "spiced Indian air, by night." Likewise, Milton in *Paradise Lost* imagined a "Pygmean race beyond the Indian mount."[94] Later, John Keats described a faery city "in midmost Ind," where a "fay of colour" resided, although admittedly this character is presented as an unhappy exception to the ruling population, being "slave from top to toe/ Sent as a present..."[95]

Doubtless 'India' had a certain exoticism for these writers and enhanced their faery theme. Nonetheless, they and their audiences had no apparent difficulty with accepting racial diversity in Faery. Comparable evidence is presented matter-of-factly in folklore reports as well. William of Newburgh, writing about England in the late 1100s, recounted the story of a man called Ketell, from Farnham in North Yorkshire, who was accosted on the road by two little black men. Although it is often the case in fairy accounts that any colour mentioned relates to the fairies' clothes, rather than to their complexion, the Latin text in this case reads "*duos quasi Ethiopes parvulos.*" The men Ketell encountered looked like little black Africans, in other words. Much more recently, some men

---

94 *Midsummer Night's Dream,* II, 1; Milton, *Paradise Lost,* Book I, lines 780–81.
95 Keats, *The Cap and Bells*, 1819, XXI.

"with black faces and wee green coaties" were seen by Jenny Rogers, wife of the coachman on the Yair Estate at Ashestiel in the Scottish Borders. Once again, they seem to have been diminutive – judging by the coats anyway – and they don't have a Caucasian skin tone. Likewise, some little people seen by men working in the fields at Strathpeffer were reported to have had "very dark skins." It seems clear we should not always make assumptions about faery ethnicity.[96]

The references in the previous section to sightings of Welsh faeries with white skin need further comment. I think it is very clear that those are allusions to a chalk white complexion, *not* to ethnically white skin, and, as such, they raise a further intriguing possibility. Many literary sources from the sixteenth and seventeenth centuries allude to faeries having faces that are coloured – not just white – but jet black, crimson, blue and green. I have examined these texts at length in my book on Tudor and Stuart faery verse, *Fayerie,* but, in summary, there is plentiful evidence to suggest that people of the period were open not just to the idea that there might be African and Indian faeries, but that they might even look radically different to ourselves, with distinctly non-human skin tones.[97]

A further aspect of the faery complexion, but one about which we have only very scattered information, is their brightness. For instance, a boy on Anglesey in the eighteenth century once saw the *tylwyth teg* dancing, and was left "dazzled as if he was looking upon the sun." This

---

96 *www.tobarandualchais.co.uk*, May 31st 1983.
97 See chapter 8 of *Fayerie – Fairies & Fairyland in Tudor and Stuart Verse,* 2020.

highly suggestive account stands almost alone, but it may be telling that in Old English women might be termed *aelfscyne,* a term that literally means 'elf-shining' but which may better be rendered as 'elf-beautiful' or even 'enchantingly bright.' Over the last century or so, the faes have increasingly come to be depicted as moving lights like Tinker Bell, but perhaps there are deeper roots to this concept. If this is so, we might be able to explain the experience of a man from Islay who was out one Sunday hunting otters. His dogs refused to enter a certain cave, so the man entered alone and was met "with a sparkling sight." He took this to be the faeries, who were warning him not to hunt on the sabbath.[98]

Eyes

Faeries' eyes are often the most noticeable thing about them. For example, one Scottish witness recalled "their wild unearthly eyes, all of one bright sparkling blue…" Another wrote that "their eyes sparkle like diamonds" in addition to which "their lips are coral, their teeth ivory…" Faery eyes are distinctive, therefore: they may be very brilliant – but they may also be extremely tiny or strangely coloured.[99]

Manx faeries' eyes are noted in particular for being distinctive: they may be very brilliant, oddly shaped or oddly coloured. One witness described their eyes as

---

98 Howells, *Cambrian Superstitions,* 138; *www.tobarandualchais.co.uk*, 1970.
99 James Hogg, 'Odd Characters,' in *Shepherd's Calendar*, 1829, vol.2.150; Crofton Croker, *Fairy Legends,* 14; W. Gill, *Second Manx Scrapbook* (London, Arrowsmith, 1932) c.VI.

being very small. However, contrast to this the experience of one Manx boy who woke up one night hungry and decided to sneak into the kitchen to steal a freshly baked 'bonnag' (bannock). Sitting before the fire, warming his hands, was a hideous fairy man with claw-like hands and staring red eyes; the child ran swiftly back to bed, still hungry. This incident is not isolated: the lost faery child found at Middleton in Teesdale had red eyes – and it's also reported that Shetland faeries are of a yellow complexion, with red eyes and green teeth.[100]

Senses

All the information we have indicates that the faeries' senses are far more acute than our own.

It appears that fairy eyesight is much sharper than that of humans. By way of illustration, a Shetland midwife who accidentally touched her eyes with the ointment meant for the faery baby she had helped to deliver found that it gave her incredibly keen vision. She was able to see ships twenty miles out to sea and could tell who each crew member was and what he was doing on board. In addition, we can probably ascribe the extreme accuracy of the elf-shot fired by faeries to their visual acuity.[101]

Fairy hearing, too, is much superior to that of mortals. They can hear over very long distances and even when the speaker is whispering. The race of faeries called the *Coraniaid* in medieval Wales were dreaded because they

---
[100] Gill, *Third Manx Scrapbook*, Part 2, c.3; Roeder, *Manx Folktales*, 16; Bord, *Faeries*, 206.
[101] Edmondston *A View of the Zetland Isles* 211; Crofton Croker, *Fairy Legends and Traditions*, vol.3, 1828, 43.

could hear anything that was said, however hushed the voice, provided that the wind caught it.

It remains the case today that there is little that is said (especially outdoors) that is not overheard by our Good Neighbours. Hence, Scottish writer, Patrick Graham, warned that the Perthshire fairies are "always, though invisibly, present; they are, on all occasions, spoken of with great respect. In general, all conversation regarding them is avoided; and when they are casually mentioned, their apprehended displeasure is carefully averted, by adding some propitiatory expression of praise."[102] Because of this constant alertness and eavesdropping, the experience encapsulated in folklore encourages us to be extremely careful about what we say: we should avoid speaking ill of the Good Folk and important secrets should only be told inside or should not be pronounced at all. The fairies' hearing is believed to be especially sharp at night (perhaps because it is otherwise quieter then or because their powers are stronger at these times).[103]

The precautions necessitated by the faeries' keen hearing include, for instance, avoiding speaking about an expected baby. This was the custom in Shropshire, so as to not alert the faeries and to minimise the risk of the child being abducted soon after its birth.[104] Not only should we avoid slandering the faeries with idle words, but, as they can overhear everything we say, we should avoid being careless in what we wish for, in case it is granted by them – to our detriment. There is in Scottish

---

102 Graham, *Sketches Descriptive of Picturesque Scenery*, 1806, 271.
103 E. Jones, *A Geographical, Historical & Religious Account of the Parish of Aberystruth*, 1779, 72.
104 Palmer, *Folklore of Shropshire*, 150.

Gaelic folklore the concept of a 'night wish' (*ordachadh oidhche*): careless words spoken after dark will be overheard by the *sith* folk and treated like a binding agreement.[105]

There is just a little evidence to suggest that the faeries' sense of smell is also sharp. In one account from the Isle of Man, a man was out late, walking across the mountains, when he came across a fine house. He was offered lodging for the night but had to be hidden when some of the little people arrive to visit. Despite being concealed inside a barrel, his presence was easily detected by the sensitive faery noses and, as soon as he'd been found, the house and all the company vanished.[106]

We do not have information about the fairy senses of touch or taste, but given what's just been said, it might be reasonable to expect that they are just as keen as their sight and hearing. Perhaps a highly sensitive palate goes part of the way to explain the fairy aversion to salt (see later).

Faeries and the Elements

One strong sign that the faeries are just as corporeal as humans is the fact that, exactly like us, they need to take shelter from bad weather. They may make do with empty barns, stables or mills, but they much prefer coming into occupied human homes.

---

105 Murray, *Tales from Highland Perthshire* no.190; Blakeborough, *Wit, Character, Folklore and Customs of the North Riding of Yorkshire*, 143; McPhail, 'Hebrides Folklore,' *Folklore*, vol.11, 1900, 441; E. Simpson, *Folklore of Lowland Scotland*, 1908, 100.
106 *Yn Lioar Manninagh*, vol.III, Part 3, 'Fairies.'

THE FAERY LIFECYCLE

Many domestic spirits, such as brownies and hobgoblins, are known for liking to sit before the fire in a human house at night. Famously, in *L'Allegro,* Milton described how one such 'lob' will be found:

> "... stretch'd out all the chimney's length,
>   Basks at the fire his hairy strength;"

Many faeries enjoy such comforts, including the Robin Goodfellow, Puck, boggarts, duergars, Manx *glashtyns* and Highland *urisks*. For most, it is part of the unspoken bargain that exists with a human farmer in return for the faery's labour.

Sometimes, the arrangements go further than this. On the Isle of Man, it was accepted that on dark and stormy winter nights the little folk would need to be able to shelter somewhere, so people would bank up their fires and go to bed early to make way for them. In Wales as well it was believed that bad weather would drive the faeries indoors. Collecting evidence in Cornwall in 1910, Walter Evans Wentz was told by one very elderly Sennen resident that *his* grandmother had always built up a good furze fire on stormy nights, telling him that the pixies were "a sort of people wandering about the world with no home or habitation, and ought to be given a little comfort." An elderly Delabole man also described the pixies as "a race of little people who live out in the fields." In the west of Scotland mistletoe has been hung over doors during frosts deliberately to provide faeries with shelter from the cold. A comparable custom in Wales is for holly to be put out in inclement weather for the same reason. In the Scottish Highlands, it is said that the *sluagh* will "shelter themselves behind little russet docken stems and little yellow ragwort stalks" during bad weather.[107]

What's more, across Britain, but especially in Wales, it's understood that the faeries prefer to wash and dress their babies in the warmth and dry inside human homes. Accordingly, wise householders will accommodate them in this with by leaving out bowls of fresh water, clean towels and a good fire in the hearth.

In all the foregoing examples a common appreciation underlies the human actions: the faeries are flesh and blood just like us and they suffer in the cold, wind and wet – even those who are reputed to be quite hairy.

Magic

Another relatively unknown subject for humans is the physiological impact upon the faery body of their magic powers. Using glamour, the faes can change their outward form – whether that is growing or shrinking or transforming into another creature or object entirely; they can become invisible, pass through solid obstacles and fly through the air.

Some of these alterations can appear quite violent: for example, it's common to hear of faeries vanishing with a flash of blue flame or, especially in the case of exposed changelings, shooting like rockets up chimneys

---

107 Moore, *Folklore*, c.3; Jones, *Appearance of Evil Apparitions*, 57; W. Sikes, *British Goblins*, 52; Evans Wentz, *Fairy Faith*, 182 & 184; J. Napier, *Folklore or Superstitious Beliefs in the West of Scotland Within this Century*, 1879, 124 & 150; *Carmarthen Weekly Reporter*, April 19th 1918, 4 'The Passing Week;' A. Carmichael, *Carmina Gadelica*, vol.2, 330.

or even through rooves.[108] It must be presumed that the faery body is designed to withstand these forces and metamorphoses although, as I mentioned earlier, it's said in Cornwall that the pixies' repeated exercise of their shape-shifting power steadily shrinks them until they become too small to see.[109]

Faery Figures

As seems to have been implied by the author of the original account of Wild Edric, his faery bride and her sisters were 'big girls' in more senses than one. We hear much about the beauty of faery women and the handsomeness of faery men, but much less about their build, although clearly for all of those humans falling for fae lovers, their bodies were likely to have been as attractive as their faces.

We *do* hear quite a lot about the physical charms of mermaids. This seems inevitable, given that their aquatic nature means that they're naked.[110] For many of the men who have seen them, their topless state seems to have made quite an impression. A mermaid seen at close quarters at Port Charlotte, Argyll, in 1857 had full breasts, a dark complexion, fine hair in ringlets and a pretty face; another sighted under the Chasms, near

---

108 Fergusson, *Rambling Sketches* 127; J. Macdiarmid, 'Fragments of Breadalbane Folklore,' *Transactions of the Gaelic Society of Inverness,* vol.26, 1905, 38; J. G. Campbell, *Popular Tales of the West Highlands,* vol.2, 1890, c.28; Gibbings, *Folklore & Legends, Scotland,* 52– 'The Laird of Balmachie's Wife.'
109 Wentz, *Fairy Faith,* 176.
110 As the old Cornish rhyme states: "Half the mermaid's human: from head to heart she's a woman;" *Passio Christi,* 1742–3.

Cregneash on the Isle of Man, had very long hair, white skin and very large breasts. A third mermaid, sadly found washed ashore dead on the island of Benbecula in the 1830s, was only the size of a child of three or four but had well developed breasts, long, dark, glossy hair and white, soft skin. The freshwater mermaid of Loch Morar, near Lochaber in the Scottish Highlands, is described in very similar terms; she had a torso "in the form of a small woman of highly developed breasts with long flowing yellow hair."[111]

In contrast to mermaids, most faery women are encountered clothed, so that the suitors' eulogies tend to focus upon their fine clothes and their hair rather than their physical charms. The faery princess Tryamour in the poem *Sir Launfal* is an exception to this, as she awaits the young knight with her upper garments shed – because of the heat, we're told... Even so, the praises are restrained, noting only her skin, "whyt as lylye yn May/ Or snow that sneweth yn wynterys day" and hair that "schon as gold wyre." There was "never non so pert," we're assured, leaving us to imagine the rest for ourselves. A faery maid discovered bathing in a forest in the *Lay of Guingamor* is "long limbed and softly rounded." Three such beauties, encountered in similar circumstances in the lay *Le chevalier qui fist parler les cons et les culs,* display their "white charms, their pretty bosoms, haunches, arms." The slim and graceful elegance of fairy women is frequently commented upon, especially in Gaelic folklore, in which there are frequent references to *bean seang sithe* (slender

---

[111] *Manx Notes & Queries,* 197–9; A. Carmichael, *Carmina Gadelica,* vol.2, 325.

faery women). These preconceptions no doubt explain why Paracelsus' term for an aerial spirit, *sylph,* was so readily adopted as an alternative word for faery and why, in due course, it acquired the sense of thin and attractive young female.[112]

Disappointingly, but probably quite predictably, we are told next to nothing about the physique of young faery men, such as the one mentioned in the first chapter who won the heart of the cow-girl on Guernsey. All we can speculate is that, given their active outdoor life of hunting and dancing, they are likely to be lithe and toned.

Faery Faces

The tendency, today especially, is to think of the fays as both tall *and* beautiful. This in part derives from the legends of the Irish *Tuatha De Danaan,* perpetuated into modern times by poets such as Fiona Macleod, whose verse drama, *The Immortal Hour,* includes the following panegyric:

> "How beautiful they are,
> The lordly ones,
> Who dwell in the hills,
> In the hollow hills.
>
> They have faces like flowers…
> Their limbs are more white
> Than shafts of moonshine…
> How beautiful they are…"[113]

---
112 Generally, see my *Love and Sex in Faeryland,* 2021.
113 Macleod, *The Immortal Hour,* Act 1.

FAERY PHYSIQUE

Another Scottish witness, Angus Macleod of Harris, eulogised as follows:

> "Their heavy brown hair was streaming down to their waists and its lustre was of the fair golden sun of summer. Their skin was as white as the swan of the wave, and their voice was as melodious as the mavis of the wood, and they themselves were as beauteous of feature and as lithe of form as a picture, while their step was as lithe and stately and their minds as sportive as the little red hind of the hill."[114]

In Wales, the accounts of the lake maidens and the girls of the *tylwyth teg* (the fair family) consistently stress their physical charms.[115] They are "fair of complexion beyond everybody," so that there once used to be certain families in the north of the country whose renowned good looks were the legacy of a famous faery ancestress. In accordance with this, folklorist Professor John Rhys reported that a fairy seen by a shepherd at Cwm Marchnad in Gwynedd was "a wonderfully handsome little woman... Her yellow and curly hair hung down in ringed locks, and her eyes were as blue as the clear sky, while her forehead was as white as the wavy face of a snowdrift... Her two plump cheeks were each like a red rose and her pretty-lipped mouth might make an angel eager to kiss her." The effect of this loveliness is highlighted even more strongly in a story from near Beddgelert: a young harpist met a fairy maid, "a little

---
[114] Wentz, *Fairy Faith*, 116.
[115] Rhys, *Celtic Folklore*, 3, 23 & 44 and 85–6 & 90 respectively.

woman who was wondrous fair beyond all his conception of beauty... The damsel gave him a jolly sweet kiss that flashed electricity through his whole nature: he was at once over head and heels in love." Interestingly, though, another Welsh story informs us that the *tylwyth teg's* own ideal of beauty is red-haired and long-nosed, whilst a further account from Lleyn presented the local fairies as "small, unprepossessing creatures, with yellow skin and black hair."[116]

Moreover, actual physical appearance seems to vary from one 'species' or type of fairy to another. Whilst it's true that some are seen as tall and beautiful women, many more look like old men and many are ugly, hairy creatures. There are certain types of faery that are renowned for being especially hideous or deformed; amongst those that spring to mind are the hirsute hobs and brownies, the notoriously small and unsightly trows of Shetland, and the spinner Habetrot, with her distended bottom lip (misshapen through years of pulling thread). For example, the sea trows have been said to have faces like monkeys, long thin bodies with huge and disproportionate limbs and heads shaped like pitched roofs.[117]

Indeed, the fairy folk not infrequently bear bodily defects that disclose their supernatural identities. For example, Highland *glaistigs* wear long dresses to cover their hooves and a few other Scottish fairies are similarly marked, so that their true natures are betrayed. Other

---

116 Rhys, *Celtic Folklore* 86, 91, 96,150 & 220; E. Owen, *Welsh Folklore*, 1896, 15.
117 W. T. Dennison, 'Orkney Folklore,' *Scottish Antiquary*, vol.5, 1891, 167.

repulsive features include a single extra-long tooth, or a malformed nose, and some Manx faeries were seen that had over-sized ears "like wine bottles." In this connection it may be significant that, in one Manx story, a young man who used to go with the fairies and be ridden by them like a horse every night, developed overlarge front teeth before he died. This deformity might be a sign of too close a proximity to the Little People. I will return to discuss misshapenness and disability in the next section.[118]

Sometimes the entire fairy population of an area is ugly (for example, Llanfabon in Glamorgan); sometimes they are uniformly tall, fair-haired and blue eyed (for instance, at Pennant, Caernarfon). Welsh folklorist John Rhys perceptively noted the anomalous fact that fairy maidens are generally beautiful but that the male changelings are usually repulsive.[119]

The folklore of faery changelings is especially informative on matters of physiology and physiognomy. Changelings are fairies who are substituted for stolen babies and Professor Rhys was right to highlight how much they seem to differ from the romantic ideal of faery good looks. Changelings have a range of identifying features, both in appearance and behaviour, which betray their origin. Wirt Sikes described the Welsh *plentyn newid,* which "has the exact appearance of the stolen infant, at first; but its aspect speedily alters." The changed child may initially look as though it has been pinched – then, it will become "generally frightful." It will be permanently

---

[118] W. Gill, *Second Manx Scrapbook,* c.VI; *Manx Notes & Queries,* 124
[119] Rhys c.XII; see too R Cromek, *Remains,* Appendix F.

hungry, yet stay thin and puny for all the food it may be given, all the while "gurning and yabbering constantly." A healthy fourteen-year-old who was taken by the *sith* folk was replaced by a youth who fell ill, took to his bed and wasted quickly away, becoming "thin, old and yellow." In the Highlands of Scotland, it is said that changelings may be recognised by their overlarge teeth and by their inordinate thirsts: they can consume a tubful of water at one meal, allegedly.[120]

From Northumberland comes a memorable summary of a changeling's highly distinctive appearance: it was "a rickety bantling [brat], peevish as a sick monkey and as ugly as sin…" Another author described changelings as looking like small, hairy and wizened old men. A unique story from Stornoway seems to confirm this description. It tells how a child was born "with the skin of an old person." The baby was cured by digging two graves on a fairy knoll – one for the living and one for the dead. The infant was laid between the two and rolled into the grave for the living. His skin healed soon afterwards. This is a puzzling and perhaps garbled account, but it seems to be about an aged changeling that is banished by a threat of death. Quite what the last report might have been trying to describe might be revealed by a fairy sighting that took place in Sma' Glen near Blairgowrie. A fairy was seen across the valley, sitting on some rocks, with what looked like a gramophone horn on its head; it was "dark, with slack skin." We should also note how, in all these cases, it was possible for these elderly faeries

---

120 Sikes, *British Goblins*, 56; Napier, *Folk Lore*, c.11; Campbell, *Superstitions*, 38; Campbell, *Popular Tales*, vol.2, 47.

to be swapped for human babies because they were the same size – underlining the diminutive stature of most of faery-kind.[121]

The shrivelled, wrinkled and ugly appearance of the changeling was one of the key identifiers of its true nature, clearly demonstrating to us the awareness of earlier generations that part of the nature of faery physiognomies was that they appeared emaciated and haggard. Our contemporary stereotype of the faery as a fresh-faced little girl has displaced, or at least obscured this, but the earlier perception seems to survive to some extent, nevertheless. Modern witnesses regularly, if not frequently, report faery faces that are gaunt or pointed and bodies that are gangly. These may perhaps be other terms to describe the same pinched and aged look recognised in the older descriptions of changelings.[122]

Lastly, whilst there tends to be a clear dichotomy in the stories between lovely faeries and ugly ones, we should recognise that certain faery types can have both lovely *and* hideous members – just like their human neighbours. For instance, some of the Devonshire pixies have been said to be "dainty beings ... of exceeding beauty [but] others are of strange, uncouth and fantastic figure and visage." One of the main distinguishing features of the pixies is said to be their pronounced squint.[123]

---

121 Oliver, *Rambles in Northumberland*, 105; Thomas, *Welsh Fairy Book*, 'Llanfabon Changeling;' Trotter, *Galloway Gossip*, 288; Horne, *Caithness*, 107; Fraser, 'Northern Folklore – Wells & Water,' *Celtic Magazine*, vol.3, 1878, 17; Rhys, *Celtic Folklore*, 83, 102 & 110; Milne, *Myths & Superstitions*, 18; www.tobarandualchais.co.uk, October 1964 and August 1955.
122 Johnson, *Seeing Fairies*, 71, 85, 115, 120, 182 & 243; *Fairy Census*, 269, 345 & 354.
123 Bray, *Peeps on Pixies*, 12; Charles Worthy, *Devonshire Parishes*,

Disability and Deformity

It can be difficult to determine the extent of disability within the faery population. One major reason for this is the natural body forms or bodily features that certain types of faery being display. For example, in the Scottish Highlands, we might encounter the *coluinn gun cheann* (the headless trunk) or the *fachan,* with its single leg, single arm and single eye. Webbed hands, overlarge teeth, outsized or hooved feet and single nostrils are all regarded as typical identifying features of fae beings. Early Gaelic tales often label bogies and other supernatural beings as *maol* or *carrach* – that is, bald, crop-eared or tonsured and scurvy or rough skinned. The Cowlugs of the Scottish Borders are, as the name indicates, a faery family with cows' ears. The trows of Orkney and Shetland are said to have long-ears high on their heads, which sounds quite similar. They are also known as 'henkies' because, as a race, they are lame, meaning that they limp or 'henk' when they dance.[124]

True disability in an individual is therefore much harder to identify. One Manx story might indicate that there are disabled individuals in the community. A couple out walking once met a small faery man begging; he was dressed in rags and had crooked legs. Whilst the wife would have helped, her husband refused to give any alms, for which he was cursed: the pair had several children subsequently – but whilst all the girls were born without

---

1887, 28; Page, *Dartmoor*, 38.
124 L. Spence, *The Fairy Tradition in Britain,* 141; *Orkney Anthology,* 1991; J. F. Campbell, & J. G. McKay, *More West Highland Tales,* vol.1, 470.

disabilities, all the boys were lame, just like the spurned beggar. Of course, in this story the beggar was one of the Little People, out in the mortal world, and he may have adopted a disguise for some reason – even if that was only to get money from humans. This motive is certainly not impossible: the English sprite Robin Goodfellow (or Puck) was known to assume the guise of a beggar purely for the purposes of having some fun at people's expense, so the Manx account does not prove with certainty the existence of physical disability amongst faery-kind. Nonetheless, we might also note the domestic sprite of the Scottish Borders called the 'wag-at-t'-wa' who looks like a "grisly old man with short, crooked legs."[125]

Suspected Scottish witch, Isobel Gowdie, from Auldearn near Nairn, in 1662 confessed to frequent contacts with the "Queen of Fearrie" and her court. Isobel had witnessed the making of elf-arrows in the "Elfes houssis" and recalled that "Thes that dightis thaim ar little ones, hollow or boss-baked" (those that shape them are small [elf-boys] who are hollow or hunch-backed). In this regard, it may be worth recording that a story common across the Highlands, and also known on the Isle of Man, concerns a hunchback who did the faeries a good turn and, as a reward, had his hump removed. Perhaps this indicates some sympathy towards fellow sufferers.[126]

---

[125] Roeder, *Manx Folklore*, 14; *Robin Goodfellow – his mad pranks and merry jests; The Ballad of Robin Goodfellow,* c.6; W. Henderson, *Folklore of the Northern Counties,* 255.

[126] Pitcairn, *Ancient Criminal Trials in Scotland,* vol.3, part 2, 602; MacDougall & Calder, *Folktales & Fairy Lore,* 205; Morrison, *Manx Fairy Tales,* 56.

Sleep

Surprisingly, perhaps, we have little information about fairies' sleeping habits. As they are a nocturnal people, active between twilight and dawn, it might be anticipated that humans would regularly encounter sleeping faes during the daytime. This is seldom the case.

Despite this lack of evidence, though, we should not conclude that the faeries don't sleep – rather, it would seem to demonstrate that they are very well concealed when they do. We have a little positive evidence to indicate that the faeries' need for rest and sleep is much like our own. The pixie boy Skillywidden, whose discovery was discussed in the first chapter, was found by the farmer when he had fallen fast asleep on a bank of heather. The faery water horses, the kelpie and the *each uisge,* very frequently fall asleep in the presence of humans. One habit of both beings is to take the form of a young man, with a view to seducing and carrying off a young woman. Often, the creature will seek to win over the girl by lying in her lap and asking her to comb his hair. Whilst she is doing this, the disguised faery will fall asleep; the girl will then discover sand, reeds or seaweed entangled in the handsome stranger's hair and will realise the true nature of her suitor. Lastly, a shipbuilder called Roderick Mackenzie, from Port Henderson in Ross-shire, one day in the mid-nineteenth century was able to capture a mermaid after she had fallen asleep on the rocks near the shoreline.[127]

---

127 J. H. Dixon, *Gairloch,* 163.

Odour

In 1650, at Dunoon on the island of Bute, a woman called Finwell Hyndman was accused of witchcraft. She was said to disappear for twenty-four hours every three months and, when she returned, she was crazed and weary and had "such a wyld smell that none could come neir hir." She wouldn't explain her absences to the community, which made it pretty clear to everyone that she had been 'away with the fairies.'

Perhaps the people of Kingarth parish were correct about Finwell. The smell that was so noticeable and inexplicable may very well have been a clear sign of her contact with the faery kind. That would unquestionably have been the interpretation placed on matters on the Isle of Man, where the characteristic smell of fairies used to be a well-known phenomenon, and was said to be pungent and strong. On Man, the upper parts of glens on the isle are reputed to be the best places to smell where the fairies have been during the night. What you will encounter is a peculiar, lingering sour odour, apparently; it is an aroma akin to the smell of a deep gill on a summer's day, we are told by those familiar with these things.[128]

That the Manx fairies seem to have a distinguishing scent is confirmed in several reports. For instance, a certain Mrs C., living in Arbory parish, one day in December 1891 went to the stream near her cottage to collect water. There was, she said, a terrible stench "between a burnt rag and a stink," and so "thick" on the

---

128 *Yn Lioar Manninagh,* vol.4. 161.

bank that she could scarcely breathe. This stench was the sign that fairies had only recently departed from the spot. A girl on the island also smelled them once – and then lost her sense of smell – although this could conceivably have been a punishment for her involuntary exclamation of "What a stink!" – which would naturally have offended the sensitive little people (her sister, who was with her, sensibly kept quiet and was unharmed).[129]

These Manx comments are echoed in an account given by a young Yorkshire woman to the Reverend M. C. F. Morris in late Victorian Yorkshire. She said that:

> "She'd never seen the faeries but she'd smelt them. What was the odour? If you have ever been a very crowded place of worship where the people have been congregated for some time, then you knew the smell."[130]

This suggests the rank redolence of unwashed bodies (even though our evidence is that the fairies are clean in their habits and bathe regularly). Much more recent evidence tends to confirm that the faeries' odour is distinctive – and possibly displeasing to human noses: encounters recorded in Marjorie Johnson's *Seeing Fairies* described an earthy or fungal smell.[131]

The odour need not be unpleasant, though. English writer John Aubrey, in his *Miscellanies* (1695), has the following record for 1670:

---

129 *Yn Lioar Manninagh*, vol.2, 194–7.
130 Rev. M, C. F. Morris, *Yorkshire Folk-talk*, 1892, c.11.
131 Johnson, *Seeing Fairies*, 33, 34 & 186; see too *Fairy Census*, 2014, no.54.

> "Not far from Cirencester was an apparition. Being demanded whether a good spirit or a bad, returned no answer, but disappeared with a curious perfume – and a most melodious twang. M. W. Lilly believes it was a fairie."

The Mr Lilly in question is almost definitely aspiring magus William Lilly, who spent much of his life trying to contact or conjure fairies and other spirits and was deeply learned in the subject. Lilly's intuition appears to be confirmed by a number of modern witnesses. Very frequently floral or sweet smells are associated with faery contacts – for example "a strange, all-pervading perfume – sweet and slightly piercing, yet flower-like and very delightful."[132]

What seems certain is that, if there is a distinct aroma at the scene of any faery encounter, it is very likely to be memorable.

Bone Structure

Logically, this subject should have been considered first in this chapter, but it is left until last because it may be one of the most obscure. Without question, generations before the early twentieth century would never have challenged the assumption that faery-kind have a bone structure exactly like ours. We have a few references which confirm this: later, for instance, we shall read about a kelpie whose leg was broken. In another example, a

---

132 Johnson, *Seeing Fairies*, 174, 190, 296–7 & 314; see too *Fairy Census*, 2014, no.290 & 326.

writer captured the distinctive look of changelings with a memorable phrase, describing them as "unearthly skin an' bone gorbels" ('gorbel' is the Scots word for a fledgling bird, evoking the scraggy chick with constantly open beak). This comparison emphasises the faery substitute's characteristically skeletal, starved form.[133] Despite this, it is true to say that the authentic remains of dead faeries have never been discovered, so that we have never had actual corpses to study (see last chapter).

Our uncertainty about faery anatomy is compounded by the fact that, since the 1920s, sightings of supernatural beings have sometimes proposed a quite different composition to their bodies to the fleshed skeletons we assume. In 1925 Geoffrey Hodson published *Fairies at Work and Play*, in which he described a succession of encounters with supernaturals across Europe. Amongst different types, he examined the elves, whose bodies, he had observed, were composed of a solid gelatinous mass. In the *Kingdom of Faerie*, Hodson further recorded that the gnomes have dark, spongy skin, which may amount to the same thing.[134] A couple of Marjorie Johnson's correspondents also reported similar observations. A Mrs Gwen Cripps of Cheshire saw a green elf, about which she remarked "I was struck by the appearance of its not having any bone structure. Rather did its body look as if made of green spongy rubber." Another individual described seeing a green wood-elf in Nottingham as a child: "its body was like shiny green jelly…"[135]

---

[133] Monteath, *Dunblane Traditions*, 54. See generally my *Middle Earth Cuckoos – the changeling phenomenon in British faery-lore*, 2021.
[134] Hodson, *Work & Play*, c.1 'Elves;' *Kingdom of Faerie*, 1927, c.3.
[135] Johnson, *Seeing Fairies*, 121 & 240.

We are left a little perplexed on the subject of bone structure. On balance, I think we must assume that faeries have a skeleton very much like our own – not least for the reason that outward evidence such as their teeth and claws tends to support such a conclusion.

CHAPTER FOUR

Faery Health

We tend to assume that the fairies are continually in robust good health, their freedom from disease being part and parcel of their very long lives or immortality. Once again, this presumption results from a failure properly to study the information we have. The reality is more complex, although this does not detract from their overall good constitutions: they live active, outdoor lives and they have good, mixed diets.

Diet

It's widely known how much the faeries enjoy feasting (and the accompanying drinking). A close study of the sources reveals that the faeries enjoy a full and varied range of foodstuffs. Some of this they raise themselves; a good deal is stolen from humans, as I have indicated earlier.[136]

A lot of fanciful, romantic nonsense is written about fairy food, much of it the product of the extreme miniaturisation of the race that took place in literature from Stuart times onwards. When the faes were reduced to tiny beings who could inhabit nut shells and flowers,

---

136 For full detail, see my *How Things Work in Faery*, 2020.

FAERY HEALTH

their foodstuffs naturally shrank too – and became increasingly dainty. Drinking nectar and dew is a common trope; poets such as Robert Herrick went further and took great delight in imagining banquets comprised of delicacies such as those offered at a banquet to King Oberon:

> "The horns of paperie Butterflies,
> Of which he eates, and tastes a little
> Of what we call the Cuckoes spittle.
> A little Fuz-ball-pudding stands
> By, not yet blessed by his hands…"[137]

These fantasies are endearing and entertaining, but they are the product of poetic fancy, not of folklore experience.

Witness accounts tend to give a very different, much more conventional description of the everyday diet in Faery. A good deal of roast beef is consumed, along with grain products (primarily breads) and milk, often processed into cream and cheese. Those little folk who live in coastal areas, such as Cornwall and the Isle of Man, will catch and eat fish – although inland faes across Britain will also take fish from rivers and lakes. It is also common for the faeries to hunt; on the Isle of Man, packs of horses and hounds are regularly spotted riding across the countryside and it is understood that a range of wild animals and fowl are eaten. Given the intimate association of many faeries with orchards, I think we can assume that fruit and nuts are consumed as well and, we should probably expect,

---

[137] Herrick, *Oberon's Feast;* see too *The Fairies Fegaries* and Michael Drayton's *Nymphidia,* Book II.

vegetables too, although the evidence on this is much sparser. We do know that the so-called 'Green Children' of Woolpit in Suffolk, who were discovered in the twelfth century, ate only green beans in the first few weeks after their appearance in the human world. In addition, the faeries are, apparently, extremely fond of mushrooms – so much so, in fact, that in Breconshire local people avoid eating them and, in Wales more generally, they are called *bwyd ellyllon* (elves' food).[138]

All of this food is washed down with alcohol (which will be discussed in a later section) and, of course, with water. Milk may be drunk too, sometimes straight from the cows' udders in the field, whilst Highland faeries are known to herd deer for their milk (and, presumably, their flesh as well).

It is very well known that the British fairies have a particular preference for dairy products. This is a taste which spans faery society, from the lowest to the highest members. The brownies, pucks, hobs, boggarts and lobs will undertake their arduous labours on human farms for fresh water and plain bread, but they love best a simple bowl of milk or cream.[139] The various Scottish Highland beings, the *gruagach, glaistig* and *loireag,* are all partial to milk and expect regular offerings of it to be made to them.[140] So keen, in fact, are fairies upon cream, milk and such like that they will notoriously resort to theft to obtain these items:

---

[138] See, variously, my *British Fairies* (2017), *Faery* (2020), *British Pixies* (2021), *How Things Work in Faery* (2021) and *Manx Faeries* (2021); Theophilus Jones, 'History of Brecknockshire,' *The Cambrian,* Dec.14th 1805, 4.
[139] Burton, *Anatomy of Melancholy* or Milton, *L'Allegro.*
[140] See my *Beyond Faery,* 2020, c.8.

> "Rude Robin Goodfellow, the lout,
> Would skim the milk bowls all,
> And search the cream pots too,
> For which the poor milk-maid weeps."[141]

In Wales the *tylwyth teg* are said to eat flummery (*ewd i llaeth*) out of egg shells, this being a sweet dish made with beaten eggs, milk, sugar and flavourings. The ingredients are, of course, stolen. The same taste for rich and delicate dairy dishes are found in the royal courts: Milton described how "Faery Mab [will] the junkets eat".[142] Ben Jonson also deployed this theme in one of his royal masques:

> "When about the cream bowls sweet,
> You and all your elves do meet,
> This is Mab, the Mistress faery,
> That doth nightly rob the dairy
> And can hurt or help the cherning,
> An' she please, without discerning."[143]

Likewise, in Thomas Randolph's *Amyntas* of 1632, fairies rob an orchard and then declare-

> "Let's goe and share our fruit with our Queen Mab,

---

141 Thomas Churchyard, *A Handful of Gladsome Verses*, 1592; see too *Robin Goodfellow – his merry pranks* and *Ballad of Robin Goodfellow*.
142 Sikes, *British Goblins*, 78; Howells, *Cambrian Superstitions*, 127; Milton, *L'Allegro*, line 102.
143 *An Entertainment at Althorpe*, 1603.

> And th'other Darymaids: whereof this theam,
> We will discourse amidst our Cakes and Cream."[144]

The faeries have a healthy appetite too and can diminish human supplies markedly. Fortunately, this can be tempered by equity and sympathy, so that poorer households may be alleviated of the burden of feeding their Good Neighbours.[145]

So great, indeed, is the fairy predilection for dairy products that it has even been suggested that they have an entirely vegetarian diet, abstaining entirely from flesh and fish. In Gerald of Wales' account of the boy Elidyr's childhood visits to faeryland, he mentions their dairy-only meals and their special preference for junkets (a mixture of curds and cream, sweetened and flavoured). Given what's been seen already, this account probably gives too much emphasis to their favourite dishes at the expense of the other items they regularly consume.

We might also get the impression that the faeries are conscious of healthy eating when we hear that abstain absolutely from salt in their food. That their motivation is somewhat different is revealed by the Cornish tradition that one way of getting the pixies to stop stealing milk directly from the cows is to smear their teats with brine; likewise, on the Isle of Man the 'little folk' can be kept away from freshly caught fish by putting a pinch of salt in the fishes' mouths.[146]

---

144 Act III, scene 4.
145 Sikes, *British Goblins*, 62 & 123.
146 Bottrell, *Traditions and Hearthside Stories*, vol.2, 73; Wentz, *Fairy Faith*, 177; Rhys, *Manx Folklore*, Part One.

Also, from the Isle of Man, we learn that the faeries don't like salt in their loaves. A woman was out walking when she heard music ahead of her on the road. She followed the sound and caught up with a group of the little people, who asked what she had in the basket she was carrying. The woman replied bread and sensibly offered to share it with them. They accepted some of her oatcakes, but only after checking that there was no salt in the mix. A Scottish brownie that had helped a family by always granting their (modest and realistic) wishes turned against them and ensured they lost everything after they had offered him salted ham. These several stories are *not* about a dislike for over-seasoned food: rather, the faeries have a physical aversion to salt and, as a result, it is regularly used by humans as a tried and tested defence against their incursions and depredations.[147]

The fairies also object to any milk product that comes from cows that have grazed upon the herb *mothan* or pearlwort. The reason for this distaste is unknown, but it is absolute – and can extend to protect any people who've consumed the milk and to the cattle that have eaten the plant. The mere presence in a room of products made from *mothan*-grazed milk can be enough to repel faeries, so powerful is its influence. We should probably

---

147 *Proceedings of the Isle of Man Natural History & Archaeological Society,* vol.1, Jan.1889; *www.toberandualchais.co.uk,* Feb.16th 1979. There is one contradictory story – a tale from Wigtown in which a faery woman borrows salt from her new human neighbour – but this may simply be a stratagem for establishing a relationship of friendly obligation (*Legends of Scottish Superstition,* 1848, 30–2 or D. MacRitchie, *Testimony of Tradition,* 1890, 115–116).

regard both salt and *mothan* as poisonous, or at least indigestible, for faery-kind.[148]

By and large, though, the faery diet is identical to that of their mortal neighbours. Poets and playwrights have given us a rather distorted view of this – witness, for instance, Shakespeare's *Cymbeline,* in which it is said of Imogen "But that it eats our victuals, I should think/ Here were a fairy."[149] Setting aside these imaginative sources, the folklore accounts show that fairies can perfectly happily eat our food and that we can eat theirs. For humans, problems might arise from ingesting fairy products in fairyland, but that is to do with magic and is nothing to do with the actual composition of the dishes. They are not poisonous for us, but they might be imbued with glamour. Positive proof of this comes from the fact that it is not harmful to eat faery food in the mortal world, whilst at the same time, as has been stressed, the faeries consistently and greedily eat our food, either here or in their own homes.

Excretion

Very little is known about the faery digestive system. It is assumed to be very much like our own – and this may not be unreasonable. They can, by and large, eat our food without any ill-effects, although we may wish to remember here the lost trowie boy on Shetland mentioned in the second chapter who was taken in by a human family and given milk – which made him vomit.

---

148 MacGregor, *Peat Fire Flame,* 274; Gregor, *Notes on the Folklore,* 136; Grant Stewart, *Popular Superstitions,* 136.
149 Act III, scene 6.

Whatever the exact details, this reaction to a disagreeable food doesn't sound too dissimilar to humans.[150]

What about the waste products of digestion, though? As mentioned in the last chapter, we have never come across any faery skeletons, neither has anyone identified faery faeces. We have a couple of clues on the matter, all the same. Firstly, it is very common to be advised in the south-west of Britain that you shouldn't gather brambles after Halloween, because the pixies have 'been over' them: in other words, they have either urinated or defecated on the fruit. Secondly, a changeling child seen on the Isle of Man during the early eighteenth century was reported to have lived with a family for nine years, "in all which time it ate nothing except a few herbs, nor was ever seen to void any other excrement than water."[151]

Intoxication

Describing the Welsh brownie-type sprite called the *bwbach,* Wirt Sikes observed how the creature always "had a weakness in favour of people who sat around the hearth with their mugs of *cwrw da* [good ale] and their pipes…" Exactly like their human neighbours, the faeries enjoy good company and all the bodily pleasures that enhance that: warmth, comfort and a mild intoxication.[152]

There is very little doubt that the faeries enjoy alcohol. They are known to make cider and to brew beer

---
150 Nicolson, *Shetland Folklore,* 83.
151 Waldron, *Isle of Man,* 1737, 30–39.
152 Sikes, *British Goblins,* 31.

(including the famous heather ale of the Highlands).[153] That they brew with yeast is not at all surprising given their well-known baking skills. The faeries' preference for a good strong pint of ale is confirmed in an amusing anecdote from Alves, in Moray in Scotland. The local minister there was told that it was tea that had driven the local faeries away. Previously the people had celebrated special occasions with beer, but the influence of the church and the temperance movement led to a switch – and to the deep unhappiness of the elves.[154]

Absolute proof of the faery liking for alcohol comes from Shetland. At Yule there was a tradition for the trows to appear and to go freely from human home to home. One trow visited a large number of houses, stealing a drink at each as he went. He ended up, naturally, highly inebriated and fell asleep in a house on the island of Yell, stretched out the bedroom window sill. The occupants discovered him there and tried to catch him, but he was able to fend them off and make his escape.[155]

There is also consistent evidence that the faeries enjoy smoking. Most often, it has to be said, such reports relate to pixie or 'gnome' types and the image of a white haired and bearded character with a pipe in his mouth has become something of a stereotype.[156] Still, so well established is the association of pipe-smoking with faeries that fragments of very early (Tudor period) clay pipes have long been

---

153 Bottrell, *Traditions & Hearthside Stories*, vol.2, 95; King, 'Folklore of Devonshire,' *Fraser's Magazine*, vol.8, 1873, 781; *The Standard*, July 24th 1873, 4 'Dartmoor.'
154 'Teas and Fairies,' *The Welshman*, October 22nd, 1858, 8.
155 *www.tobarandualchais.co.uk*, Dec.18th 1972.
156 'Pixies of Devonshire,' *Newcastle Courant*, December 25th 1846, 3.

regarded as faery pipes because of their diminutive size; they are called *cetyn y tylwyth teg* in Welsh.[157]

Cleanliness

Faery-kind know as well as we do that bodily health can be improved or maintained by regular washing, both of themselves and of their clothes.

Bathing faes

There are plenty of reports that demonstrate that fairies will regularly and habitually wash themselves. As an outdoor people, living in woods and meadows, a lot of this bathing takes place in natural bodies of water. For example, in Northamptonshire certain 'faery pools' are known where the faeries swim at night; at Brington, in fact, bathing faeries were seen by witnesses as recently as 1840.[158]

In light of this, it's inevitable that encounters with fays are likely to occur at these places. A Northumberland tale records how a little girl gathering primroses by the River Wear came upon some faeries bathing. In revenge for this invasion of their ablutions, she was abducted by them that same night and her father then had to follow a very complex ritual to be able to recover her. I mentioned earlier the red-eyed faery girl who was found lost and alone near a well-known faery bathing place at Tower

---

157 E. Owen, *Welsh Folklore*, 1896, 109; G. Herbert, 'Devonian Folklore Illustrated,' *Devonshire Association for the Advancement of Science, Literature & Art*, vol.2, 1867, 80.
158 T. Sternberg, *Dialect and Folklore of Northamptonshire*, 136; P. Hill, *Folklore of Northamptonshire*, 149; Roberts, *Folklore of Yorkshire* 64; *County Folklore* vol.2 130.

THE FAERY LIFECYCLE

Hill, Middleton-in-Teesdale. In Wales, the *tylwyth teg* were known to bathe in the pool beneath the waterfall at *Yscod y Rhyd* near Neath; in the north at Dolgellau, a pool on the edge of the town was renowned for being favoured on summer evenings, when the local people would avoid it out of respect to the faes. One man, however, a certain Hugh Evans, wanted to see a faery maiden naked and spied on a girl bathing there. This violation of her privacy interestingly didn't lead to punishment, but enabled him to take her as his wife.[159]

Over time, however, the faeries have realised that al fresco bathing isn't necessary when there are human dwellings available. The habit of entering our homes to wash must have started many centuries ago, because the provision of water has become established as – to all intents and purposes – a faery right. There is widespread testimony to this from across the British Isles, most frequently from Wales. Sometimes hot water is preferred, but very curiously, it's also reported that the *tylwyth teg* prefer to wash their children in the water in which human children have already been cleaned, whilst in the Highlands the water used for washing men's feet is most desirable. What's more, once human-kind developed their own specialist locations designed for ablutions, the faeries naturally colonised these as well, as in the widely reported incident of faes discovered bathing in the spa waters at Ilkley.[160]

---

[159] Grice, *Folk Tales*, c.15; Bord, *Fairies*, Appendix, 206; *The Cambrian*, August 21st 1891, 5 'Fairies of the Neath Vale,' T. P. Ellis, 'Welsh Fairies,' Welsh Outlook, vol.16, no.10, October 1st 1929, 297.

[160] Rhys, *Celtic Folklore* 56, 110, 137, 151, 198 & 240; Owen, *Welsh folklore*, 68; Briggs, *Fairies in Tradition*, 133–4.

Fairy laundry

Fairies wash their bodies and there is good evidence that they also do the laundry just like humans. It's worth remarking that the Ilkley faeries just mentioned were reportedly saving time and effort by bathing themselves in the spa fully clothed.

At least one spring, the Claymore well near Kettleness in Yorkshire, has been identified as a place where the faes wash their clothes and, in the Middleton-in-Teesdale case, the fairies were also said to wash dirty garments in the river Tees there.[161]

An interesting story comes from the Isle of Man in the early twentieth century. A man reported that his father, when he was a boy, had come across the fairies doing their washing in the river at Glen Rushen. They were beating the clothes on the rocks and then hanging them to dry on gorse bushes. The boy crept close and stole a little cap, which was too small even for a human child to wear. He took it home to show his mother, but she told him to go straight back and replace it – which he prudently did. In fact, on the Isle of Man both clothes washing and the bathing of children are carried out as communal activities by faery women and a number of sites are identified on the island where this has regularly been seen or heard.[162]

Unsurprisingly, fairy clothes washing moved inside human homes, too. A Shetland fisherman who had been dozing by his fire awoke to find a trow using his feet as

---

161 Roberts, *Folklore of Yorkshire* 64; Bord p.206.
162 *Yn Lioar Manninagh*, vol.4, 161 & vol.2, 194–7; Gill, *Third Manx Scrapbook,* Part 2, c.3; *Chambers Journal,* vol.3, 1855, 96.

a clothes horse for drying her child's clothes. When he moved and the washing fell in the ashes, she slapped his leg in irritation and, as a consequence, he and his descendants always limped.

Maintaining Physical Health

The faery diet and lifestyle are reasonably healthy, therefore. The sense that they are free from bodily afflictions is further enhanced by the fact that the Good Folk are widely regarded as being a source of healing knowledge and powers for favoured humans. However, what we rarely do is to take this analysis further: why is it that the faeries *are* such good physicians? It seems highly unlikely, given all that we know of them, that they would have acquired these medical skills merely to endow the occasional human with them. The only sensible explanation is that the faeries perfected this knowledge because they needed it for themselves first. Just like humans, they are subject to "the thousand natural shocks / That flesh is heir to," as Hamlet describes them.

For example, in one account from Shetland, some of the 'grey folk' (trows) were seen treating a jaundiced trowie infant by pouring water over it. A human stole the bowl that was used for this and was then in turn able to use it to cure jaundice in humans. In another story, ointment is stolen from the trows which proves efficacious for healing any human injury. In a third Shetland story, a sick man lying in bed was visited by two trows with a 'pig' (a stone bottle). They debated whether he would be cured by a drink from their bottle, but decided that time was too short and that they had to leave before his wife returned home. He had the presence of mind to bless himself – and the bottle – which thereby fell into his possession. It turned out to contain a never-ending supply of liquid that cured him and any others needing it. Interestingly, one version of this incident records that the bottle contained a salve which was finally used up when one of the man's daughters charged a patient for giving them a little of it. Faery healing skills are not to be supplied for profit.[163]

In a comparable story from Argyll, some faeries who fled a farmhouse in a hurry when dawn overtook them left behind a small bag containing (*inter alia*) an item described as a 'tiny stone spade.' This 'spade' (which was probably a flint arrow head), if placed under a sick person's pillow, would help predict their recovery depending upon whether or not a sweat broke out on the patient's forehead. What is particularly notable about all of these preceding accounts is that they are evidence of the faeries succumbing to illnesses and curing themselves. Although the focus is always upon the human benefit derived from the items acquired, the unspoken preliminary in all the cases is that the faeries have developed the healing skills and substances for their own benefit.[164]

Some of the faeries' medical skill unquestionably derives from their wider magical abilities. In the Argyll case just recounted, the 'faery spade' helped predict the outcome of sickness and it certainly looks as though the

---

[163] Saxby *Shetland Traditional Lore* 151–2; J. Nicolson, *Some Folktales and Legends of Shetland*, 1920, 38; www.tobarandualchais.co.uk, Dec.18th 1972.
[164] Pegg, *Argyll Folk Tales* 35.

THE FAERY LIFECYCLE

faeries' general powers of predicting the future include giving prognoses of illnesses. A Gloucestershire woman in the early eighteenth century was accused of witchcraft because she was able to tell whether a sick person would die or recover. She explained to the assizes trying her that a 'jury' of faeries used to visit her at night and would consider the patient's situation amongst themselves. If at the end of this they looked cheerful, the person would get well; if they looked sad, the disease would prove fatal. In a related incident, a man from Breadalbane near Inverness was one night going to visit a sick relative when he met a small woman dressed in green on a bridge. She asked the purpose of his journey and, on learning it, advised that his relation was already getting better – before vanishing in a blue flame. Her prediction proved to be correct. Other Highland supernaturals are said to predict approaching mortality by giving certain signs.[165]

Regardless of any prescience, though, much of the faeries' pharmacological knowledge was derived from long-experience. A sixteenth or seventeenth century document found in the library of the parson of Warlingham, Surrey, was a catalogue of "certain medicines... taught him by the fairies." It was a list of a range of common afflictions and the remedies or treatment for them. Amongst the ailments that had beset the local fairies were loss of speech, pestilence, rotten teeth, warts and blood loss from wounds. Interestingly, given our preconceptions about fairy beauty, there were also

---

165 John Beaumont, *A Treatise of Spirits,* 1705, 104–5; J. Macdiarmid, 'Fragments of Breadalbane Folklore,' *Transactions of the Gaelic Society of Inverness,* vol.26, 1905, 38; *Old Statistical Accounts of Scotland,* vol.21, 1799, 148.

various cosmetic preparations to deal with freckles, red faces, baldness and "to make faces fair." The prescriptions involved the use of blood and a lot of plant products, including wormwood, ivy, spurge, peach kernels, gourd seeds, bean blossoms and southernwood.[166]

Sometimes fairies will act as doctors to human kind, applying their skills directly to sick humans. For example, at the 'Hob Hole' on the North Yorkshire coast the resident hobgoblin who could cure whooping cough if asked; the faeries of the 'dripping cave' at Craig-a-Chowie in Ross-shire could cure deafness. The fairy well at Arisdale on Yell cured insanity. A particularly interesting story attaches to the Faeries' Well near Blackpool. The water of the well was known locally to be good for the treatment of weak eyes and, once, a mother whose daughter's eyesight seemed to be failing went to the well to fill a bottle. Instead, she met a small green man who gave her a box of ointment to apply to the child' eyes and her vision was saved. Unfortunately, the mother had taken the precaution of first testing the ointment on her own eyes and had thereby acquired second sight. She was blinded by the fairy man for this presumption, her apparent offence being to apply the curative ointment to someone other than the person for whom it was intended. Nevertheless, we can again infer from all these examples that whooping cough, deafness, mental disturbance and weak eyesight are all prevalent in the faery community, hence the healing knowledge they had amassed.[167]

---

166 G. L. Gomme, 'Popular Superstitions,' *Gentleman's Magazine*, vol.3, 1884, 155.
167 Spence, *The Fairy Tradition in Britain* 156.

THE FAERY LIFECYCLE

From time to time, too, the Good Folk will willingly and deliberately transmit their healing knowledge to humans. A very well-known example which I have already mentioned is that of the faery wife of Llyn y Fan Fach, who taught her half-human children her healing skills, thereby founding the renowned lineage of the physicians of Myddfai. On Shetland we hear of a faery wife who taught her human husband cures. Healing ability may also be bestowed as a gift to a favoured individual who has helped a faery being. In the Cornish story of the old man of Cury, the hero of the title rescues a mermaid stranded by the tide and, in gratitude for carrying her back to the sea, she offers to give him any three things he cares to request. Creditably, he asks, not for wealth, but for abilities that will benefit his community, such as the skill to charm away sicknesses. The mermaid taught him how to treat a range of diseases – "shingles, tetters, St Antony's fire, and St Vitus's dance; and he learnt also all the mysteries of bramble leaves…" Secondly, from lowland Scotland, comes a similar story of a woman who won favour by nursing a faery child. She was rewarded with several gifts, amongst which were the recipes for salves for restoring human health. A mermaid captured on Skye was only released after granting her captor three wishes, one of which was the ability to cure scrofula.[168]

---

168 Aitken *Forgotten Heritage* 14; R. Hunt, *Popular Romances of the West of England,* vol.1, 149–5; Dalyell, *The Darker Superstitions of Scotland* 28; MacGregor, *Peat Fire Flame,* 106. The illnesses mentioned have a variety of causes, arising from viral or bacterial infection, fever and fungal poisoning.

Sometimes, this medical knowledge is bestowed entirely freely, perhaps out of pity for the human condition. In one Scottish case, a mermaid surfaced from the River Clyde to see the funeral of a young woman passing by on the shore at Port Glasgow. She called some good advice:

> "If they would drink nettles in March
> And eat mugwort in May,
> So many braw (healthy) maidens
> Would not go to the clay."

A very similar story has a happier outcome because the mermaid tells a sick girl's lover about the mugwort remedy in good time; he takes her advice, makes a juice from the flower tops, and saves his beloved.[169]

A selkie mother advised her half-human children to "Never drink sea-water without putting it through a sieve, as there is many a living creature in the ocean." This isn't so much medicinal advice, but it definitely seems to be a good food hygiene tip, which could avoid all sorts of food-poisoning risks.[170]

These folklore accounts are consistent with testimonies from witch trials that describe faeries teaching their healing skills to humans. For example, Jonat Hunter of Dundonald was said in 1604 to have gone "with the fair folk," from whom she received the recipes for healing potions. John Gothrey of Perth was carried off to Faery as a boy and, when he returned home, he had healing powers, which were supplemented monthly by a fairy

---

169 Briggs, *Dictionary of Fairies*, 289.
170 Polson, *Our Highland Folklore Heritage*, 78.

boy who visited him to show him what herbs could be used to treat different ailments.[171]

Finally, we must note that the faeries' healing skill isn't always infallible and that sometimes they will need human aid. We know already that childbirth is a process in which a human midwife's intervention can be deemed essential. Equally, in a story from Somerset, an old woman with healing skills and medicinal knowledge was called away to attend a pixie's wife when her own peoples' remedies had been exhausted and it seemed that nothing more could be done for her. The woman looked after the pixie morning and evening for a long period until she was completely recovered, after which she was very well paid for her dedication to duty.[172]

Herbs

As a primarily rural people, it is far from surprising that the fays tend to use commonly found plants to make their potions. Frequently we're only told that "divers green herbs" are used to make drinks and salves. For example, in Enys Tregarthen's story *The Pisky Purse* she describes "herbs and flowers wet with fairy dew" being gathered to make eye salves and other ointments, but we aren't given any more detail than this. The 'green herbes' used by Bartie Paterson of Dalkeith in 1607 are another instance of this frustrating vagueness.[173]

Fortunately, we are sometimes given much more useful detail. The suspected witch, Isobel Watson of Stirling,

---

171 *Dundonald Parish Records*, 15, 51 & 64; *National Archives of Scotland*, ms CH2/299, page 422 (1642)
172 Mathews, *Blackdown Borderland*, 59.
173 Robert Law, *Memorialls*, 1690, li.

FAERY HEALTH

had met the 'fair folk' and seems to have learned from them how to use rowan in a cure for worms; Elspeth Reoch, from Kirkwall on Orkney, was taught remedies by a fairy man when she was about twelve years old and used yarrow to cure nosebleeds.[174] Bessie Dunlop, of Dalry in Ayrshire, learned a variety of herbal cures from a fairy man. He gave her something like the root of a beet and told her either to cook it, and make it into a salve, or to dry and powder it. The latter preparation was presumably ingested – and we might wish here to note the story from East Yorkshire that tells of a medicinal 'white powder' provided by the fairy queen to a local healer. Bessie Dunlop also made an expensive drink of ale and exotic spices such as ginger, liquorice, cloves and aniseed. During her examination in court in 1576 she added that if the patient "sweated out" the treatment, they would not recover.[175]

In 1597 four Edinburgh women were tried for alleged witchcraft and for being associated with the "Farie-folk.' They appear to have been traditional healers, claiming to have been taught their remedies by the Good Neighbours. Christian Lewinstoun, for example, mixed fresh butter with a 'sweet wort' and bathed one patient in woodbine and resin. She treated heart disease by seething broom and chamomile in white wine. Christian also, much less wisely, prescribed mercury (as a salve and a drink) to at least two sick people. Another of the group, Jonet Stewart, advised bathing in red nettles and alexanders; she also made a salve by seething

---

174 Black, *County Folklore*, vol.3, 1903, 111.
175 Pitcairn, *Ancient Criminal Trials*, vol.1, 49–58; *County Folklore* vol.6, 55.

alexanders in butter. It would appear that these women had acquired a good understanding of the therapeutic qualities of many common herbs; sadly, in sixteenth and seventeenth century Britain, such knowledge was too readily regarded as sorcery. The various medicinal herbs that have been recommended by the faeries are reviewed in an appendix.[176]

Another alleged witch, Alesoun Peirsoun, treated as distinguished a patient as the Bishop of St Andrews for trembling fever, palpitations, weakness in the joints and the flux with a herbal ointment which she rubbed into his cheeks, neck, chest, stomach and side. Alesoun herself had been cured of debility by the fairies and was then taught her medicinal skills by them. She spent seven years visiting the faery court of Elfame where she had seen the 'good neighbours' making their salves in pans over fires, using herbs they had picked before sunrise.[177]

Certainly, the remedies recommended by faeries all tend to be simple, traditional herbal preparations, although to gain full efficacy, these might need to be combined with precise ritual. As an illustration, the nettles which were used to treat 'trembling fevers,' had to be gathered before sunrise on three successive mornings.

Food

The herbal remedies just discussed are often hard to separate from those involving food stuffs, some of which were everyday ingredients, whilst others were rather more expensive and harder to come by. For instance, Alesoun Peirsoun also treated the Bishop of St Andrews

---
[176] Pitcairn, *Ancient Criminal Trials,* vol.2, Part 1, 25.
[177] Pitcairn, *Ancient Criminal Trials,* vol.1, Part 3, 161.

with a medicinal broth made from ewe's milk, woodruff and other herbs, claret and the liquor of a boiled hen, which he had to drink over two successive days – a quart at a time. Bessie Dunlop made a similar preparation. She was approached for help by a young gentlewoman who suffered from 'cold blood' and fainting fits, for which she prescribed a potion made from the spices mentioned before mixed in strong ale and taken with sugar in the mornings before eating.

Water

Water from certain springs and wells can have magical properties and these can cure illness if the water is either drunk or used for bathing. As we've already seen, there are several accounts from Shetland of trows using 'kapps' (wooden bowls) to pour water over patients during healing ceremonies. Both the implement and the liquid seem to have been important in the curing process.[178]

The healing power of fresh water is very often employed in the fairy-taught healing procedures. Margaret Alexander from Livingstone regularly communed with the fairies and used well water combined with charms to cure sick people. Isobel Haldane, who lived in Perthshire, also took water from wells and burns and in it washed the shirts of her patients. Her friend Margaret Hormscleugh likewise learned from the fairies how to cure people with south-running water. A woman called Jonet Boyman from Edinburgh would also diagnose sickness using a patient's shirt, which she would take to a well on Arthur's Seat just outside the city. Jonet had first acquired her healing skills

---

178 Saxby, *Shetland Traditional Lore*, 151.

by going to the same well and raising a whirlwind, from which emerged a fairy man who taught her. Margaret Dicksone, of Pencaitland, treated a suspected changeling child by washing it – and its shirt – in a south-flowing stream.[179]

Stein Maltman of Stirling had learned his healing skills from the "fairie folk," whom he often saw, and they supplied him with a repertoire of cures. He told his 1628 trial that he made several different uses of water in his cures. He would boil elf-shot in water from a south-flowing stream and either had a patient drink it or bathe in it; in one case he had a man bathe himself in such a stream having first diagnosed his illness by reciting charms over one of the man's shirts.[180]

Rituals and other items

The last category of cures involves a mixture of odd materials that were considered to have medicinal effect. Catharine Caray from Orkney, who used to meet with the fairies at sunset, was able to diagnose and cure both physical and spiritual illnesses using thread, charms and stones. For example, the thread might be tied on to the patient with an invocation of the holy trinity and the words "'bone to bone, synnew to synnew, and flesche to flesche, and bluid to bluid."[181]

---

179 A. Macdonald, 'A Witchcraft Case of 1647,' *Scots Law Times*, April 10th 1937, 77–78; L. Henderson, *Scottish Fairy Belief*, 2001, 96–97 & 127–9.
180 Alaric Hall, 'Folk-healing, Fairies and Witchcraft: The Trial of Stein Maltman, Stirling, 1628,' *Studia Celtica Fennica* III (2006) 10–25.
181 Henderson, *Scottish Fairy Belief*, 82.

Bessie Dunlop was given a green silk thread by her faery guide, Thom Reid, and she used it to assist women in childbirth. Suspected witch Andro Man, long-term lover of the fairy queen, was tried at Aberdeen in 1598. The monarch had taught Man various remedies, one of which apparently involved curing a sick man by passing him nine times through a length of yarn, and then transferring the illness from the yarn to a cat. Similar treatments were practised by Isobel Haldane and Janet Trall from near Perth, both women being healers who admitted to long-term and regular fairy contacts. After passing a person through the yarn, Trall would then cut it up into nine parts and bury them in three different places.[182]

Conclusions

We know of faery healing powers because they applied them, or allowed them to be applied, to humans. This should not distract us, though, from the fact that these skills had already been developed and perfected by the faeries in order to treat themselves. The faery population evidently suffers from almost all the illnesses that plague their human neighbours (though whether that is a result of their regular contact with us – including sexual intercourse – is an interesting matter for speculation). Certainly, the faeries' remedies must be the fruit of long-term experimentation with the resources available to them. For all their magical abilities, they still rely on plants and water for the bulk of their cures, meaning that humans can easily imitate these medicaments too.

---

182 Pitcairn, *Ancient Criminal Trials,* vol.1, 49–58; *Spalding Club Miscellany,* vol.1, Part 3, 120 & 124;

Finally, the cures used by some alleged witches and healers in order to deal with illnesses caused *by* the fairies may also indicate to us plants to which the fairies are physiologically allergic. These include the well-known rowan or mountain-ash, but foxgloves are also mentioned, as are lunary and 'sochsterrie' or fairy leaves (possibly star-grass), which was used by Isobel Haldane from Perth to drive out a changeling in 1623. Her co-accused, Janet Trall, employed a so-called 'shot star' steeped in the water that she used to bathe a baby suspected of being 'blasted' by the fairies. This substance is believed now to be an algal jelly that is sometimes found in pastures after rain. At the time, in the early seventeenth century, it was thought to be the remnants of a shooting star and, as such, to have magical and even celestial powers. Recall that our word 'disaster' originally signified the result of malign astral influences.[183]

Mental Health

It can be extremely hard for humans truly to comprehend how the Good Folk think and feel. Their perception of the world is entirely different to ours, as demonstrated by the story of the Myddfai lake maiden who cried at a wedding and laughed at a funeral. Her reactions disclosed her complete absence of recognisable emotions and her total inability to empathise with normal human sentiments. On the other hand, a Scottish account portrayed the

---

183 *Abbotsford Club Miscellany*, vol.1, 167 (trial of Katherine Craigie); John Lyly, *Endymion* (1591), Act IV, scene 3; Pitcairn, *Ancient Criminal Trials*, vol.2, Part 2, 537; *Extracts from the Presbytery Book of Strathboyce*, 1843, x & xi.

faeries as being entirely free of many human faults: they are "not limited like we are with such weaknesses as envy, hatred, spite, falsehood or intemperance." Perhaps they are paragons of virtue, but there is certainly plenty of other evidence strongly suggesting that they are just as prone to ill-temper, anger, sensitivity to criticism and vengeance as we are.[184]

Faery moods may be just as changeable as our own, and their personalities may be just as fragile and vulnerable as ours. Here, though, I'm interested in a deeper question: are faeries happy?

Some commentators and witnesses have argued strongly that they are not: there are frequent accounts of faeries agonising over their ultimate Christian salvation and this definitely suggests a profound unease and deep dissatisfaction with their state, lacking immortal souls as they do. A good example of this type of story is found in Keightley's *Fairy Mythology,* under the title of *The Fairy's Inquiry:*

> "A clergyman was returning home one night after visiting a sick member of his congregation. His way led by a lake and, as he proceeded, he was surprised to hear most melodious strains of music. He sat down to listen. The music seemed to approach coming over the lake accompanied by a light. At length he discerned a man walking on the water, attended by a number of little beings, some bearing lights, others musical instruments.

---

[184] Lewes, *The Queer Side* 126; Terrell, *Wee Folk of Menteith,* 48 & 51.

At the beach the man dismissed his attendants, and then walking up to the minister saluted him courteously. He was a little grey-headed old man, dressed in rather an unusual garb. The minister having returned his salute begged of him to come and sit beside him. He complied with the request, and on being asked who he was, replied that he was one of the *Daoine Shi*. He added that he and they had originally been angels, but having been seduced into revolt by Satan, they had been cast down to earth where they were to dwell till the day of doom. His object now was, to ascertain from the minister what would be their condition after that awful day. The minister then questioned him on the articles of faith; but as his answers did not prove satisfactory, and as in repeating the Lord's Prayer, he persisted in saying *wert* instead of *art in heaven*, he did not feel himself justified in holding out any hopes to him. The fairy then gave a cry of despair and flung himself into the loch, and the minister resumed his journey."[185]

This view of Faery seems to be very heavily influenced by traditional Protestant concepts of the nature of faeries and their place in creation. Starting from the position that they are not mentioned in the Bible, the necessary conclusion for some has been that the fairies can only be regarded as demonic. Such an approach seems to have given rise to Scottish author Patrick Graham's portrayal of the faes as:

---

[185] Keightley, *Fairy Mythology*, 385–6.

FAERY HEALTH

"a peevish, repairing race of beings who, possessing themselves of but a scanty portion of happiness, are supposed to envy mankind their more complete and substantial enjoyments. They are supposed to enjoy, in their subterranean recesses, a sort of shadowy happiness, a tinsel grandeur, which however they would willingly change for the more solid joys of mortals."[186]

As a Protestant church minister, it is unsurprising to read that Robert Kirk shared these views of the faeries' state of mind:

"Some say their continual Sadness is because of their pendulous State… as uncertain what at the last Revolution will become of them, when they are lock't up into ane unchangeable Condition; and if they have any frolic Fitts of Mirth, 'tis as the constrained grinning of a Mort-head, or rather as acted on a Stage, and moved by another, rather than cordially comeing of themselves."[187]

According to these interpretations, as the fairies are not going to heaven, they must be perpetually depressed and desperate. I'm mistrustful of the idea of Faery as being envious of humans and constantly trying to imitate us. From a Christian perspective, the fays do indeed live a sort of miserable, marginal half-life. Trows in particular have been described as "melancholy and morbid." It's not

---

[186] P. Graham, *Sketches Descriptive of Picturesque Scenery*, 1810, 103.
[187] Kirk, *Secret Commonwealth,* c.7.

at all clear, though, that they themselves see things the same way as we humans like to imagine. For example, another Scot who actually met the faeries recalled how they had whispered about him, with – now and then – "the repetition of his name, which was always done with a strain of pity." Perhaps it is us mortals who should feel sorry for ourselves: our lives are full of worries and woes whilst the faeries live a carefree existence, filled instead with dancing and music.[188]

A further Scottish writer described the fays as "a sociable people, passionately given to festive amusements and jocund hilarity." Without doubt, this is what most people believe and what you'll find described again and again in poems and stories celebrating the "frolicsome faeries" and how, for "jocund elves … In mirthful glee the hours unheeded roll." Sir Walter Scott put it most attractively: "Tis merry, tis merry in Faeryland, When Faery birds are singing…"[189]

There is, though, another possible reason why fairies might feel sad, and that is their steady retreat in the face of a seemingly inexorable human encroachment. There are several stories of the fairies departing *en masse* to escape human incursions, but what I'm particularly interested in here is the impact of these migrations upon those who find themselves left behind.[190] We get a

---

188 Edmondston *A View of the Zetland Isles*, 189; Hogg, 'Odd Characters' 150.
189 W. Grant Stewart, *The Popular Superstitions and Festive Amusements of the Highlanders of Scotland*, 1823, 90; George Meredith, *The Poetry of Shakespeare;* Charlotte Dacre, *Will o' Wisp;* Scott, *Alice Brand*.
190 See, for example, Hugh Miller, *Old Red Sandstone*, c.11 or Cromek's 'Farewell to Burrow Hill,' retold in Aitken, *A Forgotten Heritage*, 1973, c.6.

glimpse of the real experience in the following Scottish account, which is a sad report of the loneliness of one of the last faes. *The Gloaming Bucht* is a tale that's set in the Cheviot Hills near the border with England.[191] The events recounted may have happened in the late eighteenth century; they're related in local dialect.

A shepherd called Peter Oliver was working with others, gathering in ewes for milking one night, when he saw "a wee little creaturie a' clad i' green, an' wi' lang hair, yellow as gowd, hingin' round its shoulders, comin' straight for him, whiles gi'en a whink o' a greet an' aye atween its hands raisin' a queer, unyirthly cry: 'Hae ye seen Hewie Milburn? Oh! hae ye seen Hewie Milburn?'" The shepherd and his companions had no idea who this being was and were terrified. "The creature was nae bigger than a three-year-auld lassie, but feat an' tight, lith o' limb, as ony grown woman, an' its face was the downright perfection o' beauty, only there was something wild an' unyirthly in its e'en that couldna be lookit at, faur less describit: it didna molest them, but aye taigilt on about the bucht, now an' then repeatin' its cry, "Hae ye seen Hewie Milburn?"

The group concluded that the creature had lost its companion. It followed them home and they tried to feed it, but it refused their food and finally wandered off – still crying woefully, but more eerily than ever.

We have no real idea who Hewie Milburn might have been, or how the pair might have come to be separated, but this was definitely a fairy couple (as the height and beauty of the woman attest, as well as the tell-tale green

---

191 George Douglas, *Scottish Fairy and Folk Tales*, 1901.

clothes). A related report comes from Caithness: the last fairies ever seen there were said to have been a good-looking mother accompanied by a freckled child with large webbed feet. They were observed to get into a boat and sail away from the shore, never to be sighted again.

It would appear that, in the general flight of the fairies from the intrusion of human civilisation, some individuals get left behind, although we don't know whether this is because the fairies leave in haste and accidentally miss out a member of their community or because it was a deliberate act, perhaps because the stranded fairy was a nuisance or a thief. We can't be sure with the Cheviot or Caithness cases, but in another incident, from Shetland, it appears that a burdensome person might very well have been consciously abandoned. There was a fiddler called Rasnie who often played at trow dances and weddings. One day, not having heard fairy music for some time, he went to the 'ferrie-knowe' (the fairy hill) and entered. Inside, there was just one old woman remaining; the rest of the trows had fled the preaching of the Gospel on Shetland and had gone to live on the Faroes – and they had deliberately left her behind.

As the 'Hewie Milburn' incident demonstrates, the fate of the abandoned individuals is likely to be an unhappy one. Their loneliness is compounded by the fact that they are the sole remaining representatives of their kind. They are aliens in a land that was once theirs and they are left desperate and inconsolable. The possible impact of this will be discussed in the following chapter.

CHAPTER FIVE

Faery Mortality

The general view of fairy-kind is that they're immortal and indestructible. Certainly, many literary representations describe faery characters in these terms – and it's reasonable to assume that authors mostly just reflected the prevailing beliefs of their time. Nevertheless, when it's examined, the folklore evidence will be found to be starkly contrasted to this common assumption.

Fairy Immortality

Today, there is a widespread assumption that fairies, as some sort of spiritual being, *must* be immortal. There seem to be several origins for this idea, all of them to some degree external to the actual folk knowledge of faery kind. The conception derives rather from learned or religious environments, within which active speculation about faery origins took place.

From the Middle Ages onwards it has been common to draw parallels between British supernaturals and the nymphs, naiads and satyrs of classical mythology. As these latter beings were minor divinities, it was natural to transfer this quality to the closely comparable British beings. Deities are, of course, extremely rarely mortal. Another very persistent theory about fairy origins (and one which has considerable support from aspects of folklore) is to see them as the spirits of the dead or, in some imprecise way, to be associated with those deceased. They may even be the souls of our distant ancestors. If faeries are indeed the souls of the dead, they naturally cannot die again. As one of Evans Wentz' Manx informants vividly told him, "Others of the fairies are evil spirits... You can't drown devils: it is evil spirits they are, and just like a shadow on the wall."[192]

The presumed immortality of faeries was taken up by writers, as is well illustrated in Shakespeare's *Midsummer Night's Dream* (1605). The dispute between Titania and Oberon that's central to the plot arises over an orphaned human child. Titania tells us that his mother died during childbirth: "being mortal, of that boy did die." Titania had been attached to the woman so, after her death the obviously non-mortal queen took the decision that "for her sake, I do rear up her boy." Later in the play, the fairy Peaseblossom addresses Titania's new lover, the human weaver Bottom, with a cry of "Hail mortal!" It's very evident from these lines that the faeries see a stark distinction between their state and ours. Oberon seems to confirm this difference when he declares to Puck that "we are spirits of another sort."[193]

Another literary example of faery deathlessness and indestructibility comes from Thomas Tickell's verse epic *Kensington Gardens* (1758). The hero of this poem is the half-human Albion, who rules in Faery until war breaks out. During a battle with his enemy Azuriel, Albion strikes a terrible blow with his sword that severs one of his foe's

---
192 Evans Wentz, *Fairy Faith*, 123.
193 Shakespeare, *Midsummer Night's Dream,* II,1; III, 1 & III, 2.

arms and cleaves his torso from shoulder to waist. Albion thinks his opponent must have been mortally wounded and:

> "So had it been, had aught of mortal strain,
> Or less than Fairy, felt the deadly pain.
> But Empyreal forms, howe'er in fight
> Gash'd and dismember'd, easily unite."

Azuriel's arm re-attaches and he strikes the stunned Albion with a fatal blow. In Tickell's imagination, faeries were imperishable and indestructible.[194]

Perhaps there is some sort of intermediate state. The twelfth century Irish text, the 'Dialogue of the Elders' (*Accallam na Senorach*) described the *Tuatha De Danaan* as "sprites or fairies with corporeal or material forms, but indued with immortality." The Welsh *tylwyth teg* have been termed "semi-immortal."[195]

Faery Mortality

Despite the literary and philosophical conceptions, the more popular understanding, as manifested in all the folklore evidence, is that faeries aren't immortal, but that their life spans are considerably longer than ours. Their lives are so extended, in fact, that they are for all intents and purposes immortal – which probably explains the common misconception about their mortality – but they don't go on forever. Faeries will all die eventually, something the Reverend Robert Kirk expressed with his

---
194 Tickell, *Kensington Gardens*, lines 378–382.
195 C, Squire, *Mythology of the British Islands*, 404.

usual style: "They are not subject to sore Sicknesses, but dwindle and decay at a certain Period, all about ane Age." Kirk also commented, rather more judgmentally, that:

> "though they are of more refyned Bodies and Intellectualls than wee, and of far less heavy and corruptive Humours, (which cause a Dissolution,) yet many of their Lives being dissonant to right Reason and their own Laws, and their Vehicles not being wholly free of Lust and Passion, especially of the more spirituall and hautie Sins they pass (after a long healthy Lyfe) into one Orb and Receptacle fitted for their Degree, till they come under the general Cognizance of the last Day."

Indeed, Kirk seemed to suggest some idea of reincarnation or rebirth amongst fairykind:

> "They live much longer than wee; yet die at last, or [at] least vanish from that State. 'Tis ane of their Tenets, that nothing perisheth, but (as the Sun and Year) every Thing goes in a Circle, lesser or greater, and is renewed and refreshed in its Revolutions; as 'tis another, that every Bodie in the Creation moves, (which is a sort of Life;) and that nothing moves, but [h]as another Animal moving on it; and so on, to the utmost minutest Corpuscle that's capable to be a Receptacle of Life."[196]

---

196 Kirk, *Secret Commonwealth*, cc.6 & 7 and Conclusion, Question 3.

FAERY MORTALITY

English writer Reginald Scot confirmed that the faes were "subject to a beginning and an end, and to a degree of continuance." Another Scottish account of faery lifespans states that they live through nine ages, with nine times nine periods in each:

> "Nine nines sucking the breast,
> Nine nines unsteady, weak,
> Nine nines footful, swift,
> Nine nines able and strong,
> Nine nines strapping, brown,
> Nine nines victorious, subduing,
> Nine nines bonneted, drab,
> Nine nines beardy, grey,
> Nine nines on the breast-beating death."

The medieval poem, *Thomas of Erceldoune*, expressed the distinction between the faery state and ours in one simple phrase. Thomas meets the fairy queen and wants to have sex with her; she resists because she knows that this will impair her unearthly beauty and exclaims to him:

> "Man of molde, thou will me merre (mar)!"

As the queen understands, Thomas is a mortal being, born of Middle Earth, and he will inevitably return to the dust from which he came. This sharp contrast in our natures is brought out in the stories of those humans taken for many years into Faery and who, upon finally returning home, crumble into dust as soon as they touch another mortal or consume earthly food. In his account of Welsh folklore from 1896, it is fascinating to read that Elias

THE FAERY LIFECYCLE

Owen was told that, in just the same way, the *tylwyth teg* call us humans ‹dead men› or ‹men of earth.›. Humans are also sometimes called 'children of Eve,' indicative, at the very least, of our different lines of descent.[197]

There is, also, a little evidence that fairies seek to make their human captives immortal like themselves. In Fletcher's *The Faithful Shepherdess* we are told how the elves dance at night beside a well:

> "dipping often times
> Their stolen children, so to make them free
> From dying flesh and dull mortality."[198]

It appears therefore that J. R. R. Tolkien, who had read widely and deeply in folklore, understood the real situation for faery-kind. In his vision, disease and age cannot kill the elves, but they can die in battle – and therefore can be murdered. This qualified state may well seem a lot less desirable than any idea of perpetual youth and health. We find a depiction of it in another literary treatment of supernatural immortality – in Ariosto's epic poem *Orlando Furioso*. The 'sorceress' Manto explains how:

> "We are so born that all ills we sustain,
> Save only death; but you must realise
> Our immortality is tinged with pain
> As sharp as death and all that it implies."[199]

---

197 Owen, *Welsh Folklore*, 11.
198 Fletcher, Act I, scene 2.
199 Ariosto, Book 43, stanza 98.

FAERY MORTALITY

In conclusion, we humans, with our mayfly lives, will probably never be completely sure as to the truth about fairy immortality, but we can probably rely on the statement of the Reverend Robert Kirk when he said that the faeries "are distributed in Tribes and Orders, and have Children, Nurses, Mariages, Deaths, and Burialls, in appearance, even as we (unless they so do for a Mockshow, or to prognosticate some such Things among us)." Certainly, some fairy funerals have been encountered whose purpose seems, in fact, to be to foretell the death of their human witnesses and not to mark the passing of one of their own kind. Others, though, are exactly what they seem to be.[200]

From time to time, we hear of fairy funerals witnessed by humans. Such ceremonies may not be frequent, but they occur regularly enough for people to come across them periodically. For instance, a man called Richard was travelling home late at night from St Ives in west Cornwall when he heard the bells of Lelant church tolling. He saw light from the windows and peered inside; in the nave, a crowd of little people were assembled, six of whom bore a tiny bier which contained a body barely the size of a doll. The corpse was interred in front of the altar, whilst the congregation lamented the death of their queen. Richard joined in with their keening and instantly the lights went out and the fairies flew past, stinging him with sharp points. He fled – and felt fortunate to have escaped with his own life. In Galloway, in south west Scotland, a man who met a fairy funeral was asked to help carry the coffin. He took up the burden, declaring

---

200 Kirk, *Secret Commonwealth*, c.2.

that he was willing to assist – "in god's name." The cortege promptly vanished and he was left holding an empty casket; within a short period, he too was dead. Luckier was a man who met a funeral procession as he was riding home one night near St. Ouen on Jersey. His horse refused to move until it had passed completely, but he suffered no other ill effects. Katharine Briggs also reproduced reports of funerals seen at Tom na Toul in Perthshire and at Lisletrim Fort in Armagh.[201]

There are also some scattered allusions to faery cemeteries. One was believed to be at Brinkburn Priory in Northumberland; generally, in the north of England it used to be said that any green shady spot was a faery burial ground. We must therefore be very careful not to assume that these are merely patches of waste ground. In 1847 it was reported in the Manx newspaper *Mona's Herald* that a man called Quayle, living at Maughold on the island, had had his house windows broken by the faes because he had ploughed up some land never before cultivated and, in so doing, had turned up bones from an old grave yard. The faeries are well known to be fiercely protective of their privacy and to insist upon respectful treatment from humans. The violation of a burial ground will be bound to incur their wrath.[202]

Clearly, these faery burials and ceremonies must be understood as being for those who have finally reached the end of their very long lives or for those who have been

---

201 John L'Amy, *Jersey Folklore*, 1927, 27; Robert Hunt, *Popular Romances of the West of England*, 105; John MacTaggart, *Gallovidian Encyclopaedia*, 1824, 'Fairies;' Briggs, *Dictionary of Fairies*, 145 or *The Fairies in Tradition & Literature* 135.
202 Moore, *Folklore*, c.III.

the unfortunate victims of assassination and war. Scottish authority John Gregorson Campbell encapsulated everything we have learned very well: "The fairies… are the counterparts of mankind. There are children and old people among them… they require food, clothing, sleep; they are liable to disease and can be killed."[203]

Life Spans

If faeries are indeed very long lived, as opposed to deathless, is there any information that can be gleaned about their possible life spans? This is unlikely to be forthcoming during most interactions with humans, but there is one exception, which is in the practice of stealing human infants and leaving behind faery substitutes, who are generally known as 'changelings.'

If the unfortunate human parent suspects that their child has been abducted, they can try to expose the changeling before taking more or less violent steps to expel it and thereby to force the faeries to return the stolen baby. One of the most common methods is the so-called 'brewery of eggshells,' which involves a parent making a show of cooking food in empty egg-shells rather than in pots and pans. The aim is to pique the fairy's interest and to get him to reveal himself. Sometimes this may be expressed by the faery in figurative terms: "I have seen the first acorn before the oak, but I have never seen brewing done in eggshells before!"[204] Sometimes, though, the elf's exclamation is much more precise.

---

[203] J. G. Campbell, *Superstitions of the Highlands & Islands of Scotland,* 16.
[204] Briggs, *Dictionary of Fairies,* 71.

Scottish witch suspect Margaret Dicksone of Pencaitland used this method and identified a changeling who was "ane hundred years old." As we shall see, in faery terms this impostor was, in fact, a mere baby. A blacksmith of Crosbrig on the Isle of Islay lost his son to the faeries and was advised to confirm the abduction with the eggshell trick. The changeling declared that "I am now eight hundred years of age, and I have never seen the like of that before." In an example from Guernsey, a woman cooking limpets in their shells provoked the changeling into exclaiming that:

> "I'm not of this year, nor the year before,
> Nor yet of the time of King John of yore,
> But in all my days and years, I ween,
> So many pots boiling I've never seen."

In another example, the changeling claimed to be fifteen hundred years old. Plainly, faeries can live a very long time indeed before finally expiring.[205]

Accidental Deaths

Fairies can die by misadventure, as a series of examples will demonstrate. It is said that there are no trows left in the Orkneys because of a disaster that killed them all. Long ago they decided to leave the mainland and live only on the island of Hoy. To do this they assembled one night on the shores of the bay of Stromness and threw

---

205 J. F. Campbell, *Popular Tales of the West Highlands*, vol.2, no.28, p.48; E. MacCulloch, *Guernsey Folklore*, 1908, 219; Harte, *Explore Fairy Traditions*, 115 & 117.

a straw rope across the water. Just at the point that all the trows were in the process of passing over the waves, one end of the rope slipped loose, plunging them into the sea. They were all drowned.[206]

In one version of the story concerning the aforementioned faery cemetery at Brinkburn Priory, the fairy bodies are interred there because the ringing of the church's bells had killed them. The faeries are widely reputed to have an aversion to church bells; this particular story may explain why.[207]

Lastly, dramatic confirmation of the faeries' mortality comes from Dartmoor in Devon, where there's longstanding animosity between the local foxes and pixies, which has led to an ever-increasing effort by the latter to protect themselves. The foxes hunt the pixies, digging them out of their underground homes and devouring them. The pixie folk have responded by making themselves iron shelters.[208]

Faeries Killing Faeries

As we've learned, age, sickness and misadventure will ultimately overtake even faes. This is sad, but not necessarily shocking. More disturbing is the evidence that faeries can kill each other prematurely. This may happen as part of warfare or even, perhaps, as a result of predation. Fairy battles have already been mentioned; one, witnessed on Greenie Hill near Birsay on Orkney,

---

206 R. M. Fergusson, *Rambling Sketches in the Far North*, 1883, 133–134.
207 *Denham Tracts*, 134.
208 R. King, 'Folklore of Devonshire,' *Fraser's Magazine*, vol.8, 1873, 781.

was described as "an awful fight – lots of men were killed on both sides and wounded. Both armies drew off and marched back to their respective knolls, while a number were engaged in carrying the dead and wounded off the field of battle."[209]

Fascinatingly, too, we have in one case some evidence for cannibalism. It appears that a water horse that had killed a man was subsequently itself killed by other water horses in the same loch, possibly because it smelled of the human it had just consumed.[210]

Humans Killing Faeries

The opinion of the Reverend Robert Kirk was that humans seemed to be unable, in normal circumstances, to injure fairies in any way:

> "for they are a People invulnerable by our Weapons; and albeit Were-wolves' and Witches' true Bodies are (by the union of the Spirit of Nature that runs thorow all, echoing and doubling the Blow towards another) wounded at Home, when the astral assumed Bodies are stricken elsewhere; as the Strings of a Second Harp, tune to ane unison, Sounds, though only ane be struck; yet these People have not a second, or so gross a Bodie at all, to be so pierced; but as Air, which when divyded unites againe; or if they feel Pain by a

---

209 D. S., 'Greenie Hill & The Good Neighbours,' *Old Lore Miscellany*, vol.3, 1909, 211.
210 MacGregor, *Peat Fire Flame*, 75.

FAERY MORTALITY

Blow, they are better Physicians than wee, and quickly cure it."

Kirk alluded here to the common belief that a witch, wounded whilst she was in the form of, say, a hare would suffer a similar injury on her human body. However, he did not believe that the faeries had any physical, corporeal form that could be injured in the same way. He proposed instead that their bodies could reform or heal themselves (as Thomas Tickell imagined in *Kensington Gardens*) or, perhaps, that they are simply far better physicians than we are.[211]

Despite Kirk's great knowledge, though, an honest survey of the folklore reveals numerous instances in which humans are able to kill faery-kind. In fact, the knowledge of this possibility lies at the very core of the most widespread procedure for dealing with changelings. Throughout Britain, the belief is that the only sure way of recovering the stolen human child is to treat the faery substitute so badly that its family are driven to rescue it and return the abducted baby. The commonest methods of doing this are burning or drowning the changeling, although severe beatings and exposure have also been tried. These strategies can only be expected to work if it is known that the faery parents will fear that the changeling might be killed or – at the very least – seriously injured or maimed. It seems, then, that humans have long been aware of the faeries' vulnerabilities.

---

211 Kirk, *Secret Commonwealth*, c.7.

THE FAERY LIFECYCLE

The seal-like supernaturals called selkies in Scotland used to be hunted and slaughtered for their skins and blubber by fishermen. In fact, there are reports from around the British coasts of mermaids being wounded and killed as well, whether by clubbing, gunshot or by being left to die of exposure when stranded on a beach. It appears that merfolk, in their part-fish form, are unable to live for very long out of the water and will die from being exposed to the air.[212]

On the Hebridean island of Benbecula a mermaid was accidentally slain by a stone thrown at her head during an attempt by some fishermen to capture her; in a Shetland story, a mermaid who was caught up in a fishing boat's lines was stabbed by one of the crew in order to get rid of her. She sank out of sight and the hook was freed, but the man never prospered after that time. These deaths all came about because the selkies had a commercial value or because they threatened human commercial interests, competing with terrestrial fishermen for fish stocks. The latter story also alerts us to the fact that, whilst it may be possible to kill a supernatural being, there may very well be a price to pay for it.[213]

Some faery killings are committed by humans in the heat of the moment or in self-defence. There are various versions of the Scottish ballad, *Lady Isabel and the Elf-knight,* but they all culminate with the heroine either stabbing or drowning the wicked elf. Isabel only behaves in this unladylike manner because she discovers that his sole interest in her is to kill her. The Reverend Robert

---

212 E. Edmonston, *Sketches & Tales of the Shetland Islands,* 79;
 J. Rhys, *Celtic Folklore*, vol.1, 199.
213 Brand, *Description of Zetland,* 172.

FAERY MORTALITY

Kirk mentioned a man with second sight who, during a visit to Faery, was attacked – but he "cut the Bodie of one of those People in two with his Iron Weapon and so escaped this Onset, yet he saw nothing left behind of that appearing divyded; at other Times he out-wrestled some of them." In the Highland story of *The Young King of Easaidh Ruadh* the hero slays a *gruagach* with his sword (though this is admittedly by hitting a vulnerable spot on the creature's neck, marked by a mole). Additionally, these examples illustrate the efficacy of cold steel against faeries: its presence can repel them but it can also be used to destroy them.[214]

Other faery murders are just that – deliberate and premeditated killings. One case from Shropshire concerns some nuisance boggarts in a farmhouse. The story follows the pattern of the 'we're flitting too' type of tale, in which the family try to escape their unwelcome companions by moving house, only to find that the boggart comes with them. In most versions the humans reconcile themselves to their unwanted housemates and often give up the move altogether. In the Shropshire version, the household takes matters to their logical conclusion. Unable to give the boggarts the slip, the humans trick them into sitting in front of a blazing fire in the hearth and then topple them into the flames, where they're held in place with forks and brooms until they're consumed. In a Manx version, the troublesome faes are bundled into a barrel and chucked in the sea so as to be rid of them.[215]

---

214 Kirk, *Secret Commonwealth*, c.8; Campbell, *Popular Tales*, vol.1, 6.
215 Burne, *Shropshire Folklore*, 45–47; Roeder, *Manx Folk Tales*, 23.

A Highland girl exposed her handsome lover as a kelpie by spilling boiling water on his feet. He whinnied instead of yelling, in response to which her brothers stabbed the man to death. The corpse left lying on the floor was that of a horse, not a human. The incident confirms the vulnerability of faes to steel weapons, as well as reminding us that they are quite as susceptible to injuries as we are.[216]

There is even one case recorded where a faery was executed under judicial process. The wife of the chief of the Macfarlane clan in Argyll was ill and couldn't nurse her baby, so her husband kidnapped a local urisk's wife and took her to his castle to serve as wet nurse (note the reversal here of the usual roles that were discussed in the first chapter). The urisk was, perhaps forgivably, enraged by this so, in revenge, he mutilated the family's milkmaid. He was hanged on a headland to serve as an example.[217]

The mortality of other forms of faery being underline their overall susceptibility to lethal injury. There are various ferocious faery beasts whose main activity seems to be to entrap and to kill (and frequently devour) human beings. Luckily, they can often suffer exactly the same fate as their intended victims. For example, the vicious water horses called kelpies can be killed with hot iron. These creatures have a habit of infesting certain neighbourhoods, alarming or killing the inhabitants, and, in one such case, a local farmer resolved to take steps to stop his family being terrorised. He heated up two metal

---
216 A. Polson, *Our Highland Folklore Heritage*, 85.
217 H. S. Winchester, *Traditions of Arrochar & Tarbet*, 1916, 'The Goblin of Rudhe Ban.'

spits and waited until the kelpie appeared, when he plunged both into the beast's side. The marauding beast died instantly.[218]

Although they are aquatic creatures, kelpies can also, surprisingly, be drowned. There was one at Braemar which took a fancy to a human woman and wooed her by various means, including keeping her well supplied with oatmeal. The beast used to get this by stealing it from the mill of Quoich. One day the miller spotted the kelpie carrying off a sack of meal and he hurled at him a stone object called a 'faery whorl' which was used to stop the mill wheel turning at night. The whorl broke the kelpie's leg and he fell into the mill leet and perished. Other equally prosaic fates include two kelpies who were mauled to death by dogs. For such a fearsome monster, they seem surprisingly straightforward and easy to defeat.[219]

On the island of Eriska, there was once a nuisance example of the water horse called an *each uisge*. This beast was killed by an expert archer who specialised in this type of pest control – although even he needed three arrows to kill this particular one.[220] The Scottish water bulls (*tarbh uisge*) are reputed to be invulnerable, except to silver shot.[221] That said, there is also report from the island of St Kilda of a man who slew one with a bow and arrow. The Manx form of the beast seems to be just as

---

218 Gregor, *Notes on Folklore*, 66.
219 McPherson, *Primitive beliefs*, c.4; Dempster, "Folklore of Sutherlandshire," *Folklore Journal*, vol.6, 223, 224 & 229; W. Gregor, "Kelpie stories," *Folk-Lore Journal*, 1883, vol.1, 293.
220 "Faery Tales", *Celtic Review*, vol.5, 166; MacGregor, *Peat Fire Flame*, 75; Campbell. *More West Highland Tales*, 206.
221 J. MacCulloch, *The Highlands & Western Isles of Scotland*, (London, Longman & Green, 1824), vol.4, 330.

THE FAERY LIFECYCLE

strong but just as vulnerable: whilst sticks and pitchforks cannot harm them, a shotgun or rifle will be effective.[222]

Humans can also kill faeries unwittingly and unintentionally. From Sutherland comes the story of a Braemore man whose wife was taken by the faeries whilst she was going to visit some neighbours. A woman looking exactly like the man's wife returned home after the visit, but she was subtly different to before, seeming more efficient and accomplished in all her household chores. However, she sickened and died after only a year. Eventually, the man's real wife was able to escape and come home and it became clear that she had been, at first, replaced by an old faery woman, a sort of adult changeling. However, faeries can only survive in human form for a year – hence the replacement wife's death.[223]

Related, perhaps, is the North Yorkshire case of a faery baby found once in a field during hay making. Although cared for by the finders, before the day was out the child had dwindled away until it was gone. Likewise, the North Midland water spirit called the asrai melts away in the light if she is caught by a fisherman and hauled into his boat from the pool in which she lives. In the Suffolk story 'Brother Mike' a faery is captured stealing corn from a farmer's barn. The captive is tethered to the farmhouse kitchen window and there he sickens and dies, having refused all food. This last fatality might have been

---

[222] Dalyell, *Darker Superstitions*, 545; MacGregor, *Peat Fire Flame*, 80; Gill, *Second Manx Scrapbook*, c.VI; Waldron, *Isle of Man*, 43; Roeder, *Manx Folktales*, Part One.
[223] G. Sutherland, *Folklore Gleanings ... from the Far North*, 1937, 23–24

accidental on the part of the captor, but it might also be viewed as a deliberate act by the despairing faery.[224]

Suicide

Fairies can be killed by their own kind and by humans. It remains to be acknowledged, sadly, that they can also kill themselves. This seems to happen in the sort of circumstances of abandonment and despair that were described at the end of the previous chapter.

The story of the 'Fairies' Gallows' from Guernsey describes this situation most fully. The fairies living in the north of the island faced displacement by witches wielding evil magic. There was a sacred spring running from the foot of a granite outcrop at Fontanelle Bay, the waters of which had magical properties. If they were drunk, the drinker would be unable to remember the past. Feeling increasingly harassed and unhappy, the local *faiteaux* decided to gather at the spring, drink the enchanted water and forget all their accumulated sorrows. Regrettably, they discovered that, as supernatural beings, they couldn't benefit from the spring's magical properties. They concluded that their means of only escape was death, so they all trooped to the top of the nearby hill called *Hougue Patris* and hung themselves with lengths of grass. No fairies were ever seen again in the vicinity.[225]

On Jersey, too, the fairies are said to have hung themselves *en masse* at Noirmont. A lone fairy man was

---

224 Atkinson, *Forty Years in a Moorland Parish*, 54; Briggs, *Dictionary of Fairies*, 'Asrai;' Kruse, *Beyond faery*, 2020, 59–61; F. Young, *Suffolk Folklore*, 128–131.
225 Marie de Garis, *Folklore of Guernsey*, Part V.

later said to have been seen suspended from a cabbage stalk, one of the very last of the *petit faitcheaux* on the island.[226]

Contrary to our expectations, therefore, faery life is not one endless round of feasting and pleasure. They are as prone as humans to depression and despair – a sobering and perhaps unwelcome thought, but a fact nonetheless.

Earthly Remains

The last issue for us to consider is this: when a fairy dies, what mortal remains are left behind? In my introduction, I noted the alleged faery body found in 1902, the desiccated mummy of a nearly intact corpse. This, and the Cornish account of the faery queen's funeral at Lelant notwithstanding, the faerylore tells us that what we should expect to find is surprisingly different to our automatic assumptions of a body in a coffin.

Before proceeding, we should recognise that an exception has to be made here in respect of mermaids and selkies. Readers may recall that a number of dead merfolk have been found, washed ashore around the British coastline. It is not at all clear why the situation appears to be different between merfolk and faeries. The best explanation would seem to be that mermaids and selkies, in their different ways, span the species: they can be both sea creatures and humans. As a result, their bodies would appear to share something of the mortal element of fish and sea mammals.

---

226 Simon Young & Ceri Houlbrook, *Magical Folk*, 2018, 155.

FAERY MORTALITY

A little earlier, I described how a Scottish farmer managed to kill a kelpie with two red hot iron spits. When the creature died, we are told, it dissolved into "a heap of starch, or something like to it." Of this description, faery authority Lewis Spence observed that it "may be accepted as providing a popular notion of the composition of supernatural bodies."[227] Such an outcome is, in fact, not unique in the records.

On the Scottish island of Raasay a blacksmith, whose daughter had been abducted and killed by an *each uisge*, managed to trap and kill the monster using two lengths of heated iron. When he inspected the corpse of the animal afterwards, he said it resembled only grey turves or a soft mass like a jelly fish. A closely related account concerns a man from Tubernan, in Sutherland, who made a bet that he could catch the kelpie that haunted the loch of Moulin na Fouath and afterwards take his bound prize to the inn at Inveran, near Lairg, to boast of his achievement and to collect his winnings. Equipped with a dog to help in cornering the beast, and an iron needle and awl to help subdue it, the man succeeded in his mission and threw the trussed-up corpse across his horse so that he could take it to the inn to display in triumph. However, when the party arrived there, the kelpie had (again) dwindled away to nothing but a lump of jelly. A third example is that of the kelpie in human disguise who was exposed by boiling water and then stabbed to death by a girl's brothers. As stated earlier, the murdered man firstly looked like a dead horse, but

---

227 Gregor, *Notes on Folklore,* 66; Spence, *The Minor Traditions of British Mythology,* 20.

the body quickly melted away to nothing but slime. Something very similar happened when a Manx man was cutting turf one summer evening in the 1820s. He saw a water bull (*tarroo ushtey*) rise out of a well and grow bigger and bigger and, gripped by panic, the man set about the beast with his spade, until there was nothing left at all but a soft jelly, like frog-spawn. Finally, on the Shetlands, a homicidal trow used to haunt Windhouse on Yell. He appeared one night when a shipwrecked sailor was sheltering there. When the trow, looking like a black lump, woke the man with a terrible roar, he responded by throwing an axe at the creature, which collapsed into a heap of blubber.[228]

Very few faery cadavers have ever been found, but perhaps the reason for this is that we have never identified the remains for what they really are.

---

[228] J. G. Campbell & McKay, *More West Highland Tales*, vol.1, 209; J. F. Campbell, *Popular Tales*, vol.2, 204; A. Polson, *Our Highland Folklore Heritage*, 85; Gill, *Manx Scrapbook*, c.1; *www.tobarandualchais.co.uk*, Sept.20th 1970.

Conclusions

To summarise, therefore: the anthropoid faeries not only look like human beings but, in many key physiological respects, very closely resemble us. They share our diet; they seem susceptible to the very same diseases and can be treated with the same medicines; they can interbreed with us so that faery women can bear half-human children and *vice versa*.

The faeries' life spans may far exceed ours, but they will eventually wither and die in the natural course of events. More significantly, they can die prematurely because of violence, being as vulnerable to wounds and trauma as any human being.

There is, though, much that we still don't know. We assume that the fairies' perspiration, respiration and circulation are the same as ours, but there is very little proof – other than those cases where we know that fairy blood has been shed, which have been mentioned earlier.[229] It remains very far from clear whether the different types of faery – brownies, boggarts, pixies, elves and so on – are entirely different species or whether they are just races of a single genus, showing outward differences but with almost no genetic differentiation.

---

[229] See too McCulloch, 'The Folklore of the Isle of Skye,' *Folklore*, vol.33, 1922, 206

There are gaps too in our knowledge of faery diet and nutrition. Given that they are a people who largely dwell underground and usually only appear at night, we might be concerned about their levels of vitamin D as they so rarely see the sun. Evidently, faery biology has some marked differences to human, despite many superficial resemblances.

There is still much for us to learn. A familiarity with faery kind of over one thousand five hundred years has not revealed everything to us. Only continued close contact will answer our many questions.

APPENDIX

A Note on Faery Herbs

The chapter on faery health included quite an inventory of herbs and plants utilised by the faes in healing. Some indication of the breadth and depth of their knowledge may come from briefly analysing those mentioned.

- Alexanders can promote appetite, aid digestion and act as a mild diuretic and disinfectant;
- Aniseed aids digestion and can be expectorant and aphrodisiac;
- Blackberry reduces menstrual pain, is a tonic for the blood and kidneys and can treat eczema;
- Broom has purgative and diuretic properties; it has also been used to treat heart disease and cancer;
- Chamomile is anti-inflammatory, analgesic and disinfectant;
- Cloves are antiseptic and numbing and aid indigestion;
- Ginger suppresses nausea, helps digestion and reduces fever. Inhaled, it can treat lung infections;
- Gourd seeds may contain valuable chemicals active against several diseases;
- Ivy is a blood cleanser, tonic and diuretic as well as

being an expectorant and a treatment for bruises and inflammations;
- Liquorice is an expectorant, diuretic and laxative. It reduces inflammations, detoxifies the liver and strengthens the immune system;
- Mugwort aids digestion and menstrual pains and treats skin problems;
- Nettles are diuretic and clear uric acid from the body. Applied externally, they can reduce inflammation and treat eczema and wounds. The seeds are used to treat tuberculosis and bronchitis;
- Peach leaves treat whooping cough and intestinal parasites; the stones have digestive benefits;
- Rowan, whilst it may repel faeries, is a rich source of vitamin C and can be used as a gargle for thrush;
- Southernwood is a tonic and expels worms. Used externally, it can treat skin conditions;
- Spurge has been used to treat warts, verrucae, corns and ringworm;
- Woodbine, or honeysuckle, has been used to treat urinary disorders, headaches, diabetes, arthritis, and cancer. It has also been used as a laxative and contraceptive;
- Woodruff is diuretic and sedative and relieves stomach pains;
- Wormwood is a digestive tonic, treats fevers and expels worms;
- Yarrow has numerous uses: it can be consumed as a tonic, as a diuretic and to reduce blood pressure. The leaves, applied as a poultice, stop bleeding and treat eczema.

www.ingramcontent.com/pod-product-compliance
Ingram Content Group UK Ltd.
Pitfield, Milton Keynes, MK11 3LW, UK
UKHW042331020625
459219UK00005B/40